TRAINING MISSION

There were only five Hyos fighters, perhaps an advance party for some swarm. Indiw picked one out, cut it off from its fellows, and told Falstaff, "That one's ours. Your turn to lead, Pit Bull Three."

It was a hard fight. The Hyos swooped and dodged and delivered resounding blows with their impulse cannons. A Hyos missile streaked toward Falstaff's tail. Falstaff dodged, and Indiw got the missile, but the Hyos matched Indiw's maneuver and pounded his shields.

Falstaff returned, slamming the Hyos with his cannon. Indiw twisted free and dove under them, stealing a split second to check the auto-scanners for other Hyos. He couldn't believe there were only five of them. . . .

HERO

DANIEL R. KERNS

ACE BOOKS, NEW YORK

This book is an Ace original edition,
and has never been previously published.

HERO

An Ace Book/published by arrangement with
the author

PRINTING HISTORY
Ace edition / October 1993

ISBN: 0-441-32802-4

ACE ®
Ace Books are published by The Berkley Publishing Group,
200 Madison Avenue, New York, NY 10016.
ACE and the "A" design
are trademarks belonging to Charter Communications, Inc.

PRINTED IN THE UNITED STATES OF AMERICA

10   9   8   7   6   5   4   3   2   1

This novel is dedicated to Debbie, without whom it would never have come into existence.

But it is also dedicated to the members of the twentieth-century American Pit Bull Squadron, without whom it would have little meaning.

Uphold the tradition.

It matters.

ACKNOWLEDGMENTS

Here I must thank Quill and Screen Services for inspiration and information, the Klein family for producing a staunch ally and best friend, the U.S. Air Force for doing their job so well (a lot better than the First Tier Alliance, anyway!), the Yonkers School District for exploring alternative command structures, and Brian Phillips for hours of painstaking proofreading and computer work. Does anyone realize the epitome of the martial arts is computer wrestling?

In addition to those who contributed to the creation of this work, there are those who have labored to bring it forth onto the bookstands: Richard Curtis, my agent, who has had such faith in my product; Susan Allison, and the veritable army of professionals at Ace Books who do their jobs at least as well as the U.S. Air Force—and a lot better than the First Tier Alliance does theirs.

★
CHAPTER
ONE
★

INDIW PAUSED IN THE DOOR OF THE HUMANS' BRIEF-
ing room, combat pilot's helmet tucked under one arm. He
wore the special goggles that transformed the light the humans
preferred into something that didn't give him a headache, but
they made everything seem unreal.

Half of the fighter pilots turned in their chairs to look at
him, nudging their neighbors. He wondered what they saw.

Indiw's flight suit was tailored to make him appear as one
of them, complete with rank insignia and squadron patch.
When the quarter master had handed it to him, Indiw had
groped deep into his memory for the text on human customs
he had once been required to study. At least he'd remembered
enough of it to know when to keep silent.

Their uniforms concealed a myriad of subtle differences so
they seemed almost like normal Ardr. He knew the proportions
of human limbs were different, their necks were improbably
skinny, and their muscle contours all wrong—he refused to
think about their soft moist skin—and of course they had no
horns or claws, but they were still people, even though you
could hardly tell which ones were female. They all stank,
which was something the textbooks didn't emphasize. He
supposed he'd get used to it.

If he wanted to fly with this fighter wing, even just this
once, he'd have to adjust. And with the Hyos still swarming,

1

there was no way he was going to be left aboard when the squadrons went out to combat. Someday, somehow, he'd get back to an Ardr ship, but meanwhile, he was going to fly no matter what it cost him.

Aware of the eyes still on him, he edged through the door and scanned the room. There were no vacant chairs. No one offered the least hint of what he should do. They were waiting to judge him on his knowledge of their protocol. That was, after all, reasonable. If he was going to take a place among them, their lives would depend on his ability to fill that place seamlessly.

He could easily imagine his own horror if their positions had been reversed and he were being asked to welcome a human pilot into his own wing. He had to reassure them.

Adopting their stiff, crisp walk as best he could, he strode down the center aisle and stood at the end of the table on the little dais. It was the obvious thing to do. Soon, someone would come to instruct them in the details of this mission, and that person should know where Indiw fit into the pattern.

He focused his eyes on the empty top of the table and relaxed into complete stillness, a battle-ready stance his martial arts instructors would have lauded. He did not even startle when a figure appeared in the doorway and simultaneously someone barked, "Ten-hut!"

Every seated human snapped to his or her feet braced into identical stances. Then there was absolute silence as the man in a shipboard uniform strode up the aisle between the chairs, his steps all the same size, his arms moving with his stride. He was one of the dark brown ones with glittering black eyes. His nose was broad, his lips sculpted. He looked far more trustworthy than the other humans in the room.

He reached the front, stepped up beside Indiw, turned, surveyed them as if memorizing their faces, then snapped, "Officers, be seated."

Everyone sat, in almost exact unison. And none of the chatter resumed. They all sat with their hands on their knees, shoulders squared to the front of the room. It was eerie. But Indiw wasn't going to let himself be spooked. He knew that unison movement was just one of the rituals humans used to create a hunting pack out of individuals who were strangers to one another. At least he knew it intellectually. His heart was racing.

He turned to the human beside him and said with utmost politeness, "You may suggest what position I might fill best." He was even willing to accept, without the obligatory polite discussions, whatever suggestion was made.

The room stirred. It was a soft susurrus of caught breathing, swallowed comments. Indiw knew instantly he'd done the wrong thing. But how? What?

The human nodded, swallowing in such a way that the bulge in his throat bobbed. "I am Captain Harsher Glass, and I command all four of the wings based on the carrier *Tacoma*. You may address me as Captain, Captain Glass, or sir."

"Thank you." Only now did he note the name badge pinned among the complex code markings on the man's uniform.

With a deep sigh, Glass paced to the edge of the platform to stand before the squadron that had the front center seats.

Indiw's helmet and flight suit bore the same emblem those four pilots wore, though the smaller one on the end had emblems that looked brighter, newer than the others'. But their squadron was complete. He didn't belong with them.

"Pit Bull, attention."

The four pilots leapt to their feet, braced in that unnatural position, eyes focused somewhere beyond the man who was talking to them.

He looked them over. Even their breathing stopped. "Commander Grummon, your squadron has the honor of welcoming Commander Indiyou to the Hundred Twentieth Fighter Wing.

We are all very pleased to have a pilot of his accomplishments among us."

Indiw got no indication that this pleasure was either real or shared. It was another liturgy, the pack leader trying to force his followers to accept a new one among them.

Well, Indiw could use all the help he could get. He made a polite bow toward Grummon, hoping it would be taken for respect. "I am most pleased to be here."

There was a general stir of laughter at that. Turning to Indiw, Glass chuckled, then said so softly Indiw thought it unlikely the other humans in the room could hear him, "Well done! A sense of humor is what it takes around here. And after all you've lost, if you can joke about it—you're okay."

Then Glass produced a data nodule from his inner pocket and held it between his fingers as he turned back to the squadron. "Commander Chancy."

The small one on the end near Indiw took one measured step forward. "Sir!"

"You will return to Search and Rescue until there's another fighter pilot opening. It's not that we don't appreciate your already proven abilities, but Indiw here will be taking the Pit Bull Four slot. Here are your orders." He handed over the data nodule.

"Yes, sir. Thank you, sir." It was a high, light voice, but the tone didn't sound at all grateful. Indiw looked hard at the human. The top front of the uniform bulged hugely. There were tiny gold devices strung through both earlobes. Though it was not definitive, men generally wore larger decorations, and then in only one ear. Her eyebrows were artistically arched, her lashes dark, perhaps artificially enhanced. Human males didn't do that. And they didn't color their lips, either. And now that he was looking for it, he noticed how her hips flared, requiring extra pleats in her flight suit that the males didn't need. Her chest and her hips seemed to have the same dimensions, while all the males boasted flat, narrow flanks much smaller than their shoulders.

This one had to be a female. Her eyes flicked once to the data nodule as she plucked it from Glass's hand, then resumed the unfocused stare over Glass's shoulder.

She snapped one hand up in the salute to a superior, retrieved her helmet from under her chair, then met Indiw's gaze straight on. "Welcome to Pit Bull Squadron, Commander Indiyou." Without waiting for an answer, she tucked her helmet under her arm and walked up the center aisle to the door. The hips were definitely a secondary sex characteristic. Very distinctive.

Indiw had heard her utter barely two formalized sentences, yet he was uncannily certain that she was furious. It was understandable. She had been displaced through no incompetence or lack, and obviously not by her own choice. If somebody tried that on him, he'd gut them on sheer reflex. And he was just a male. Imagine what a female might do. In that moment, he knew he'd made a serious mistake choosing to fly this mission.

Glass gestured Indiw to take the vacated place, then said, "Pit Bull, be seated!"

The three humans sat, and Indiw followed suit. He ended up with his flight helmet awkwardly in his lap, which forced his elbows to stick into the people crushed up close on either side of him. Human pack behavior would be irritating.

The two humans on either side of him inched away as Glass said, "Today, the final flight briefing will be provided by Captain Sutcliff since it involves matters of higher level policy." With that, Glass strode up the aisle and out the door.

The moment he crossed the threshold, the room erupted in movement and sound. People twisted around to talk to their neighbors, or even got out of their seats to speak to someone farther away. Others turned on the units built into the folding arm of their chairs to view the briefing data.

Indiw took that opportunity to stow his helmet under his seat. He'd already wrung everything he could out of the ship's data systems on the upcoming mission.

The man next to him—the hair over his mouth signified male—leaned over and said, "You'll be my wingman, then. I'm Falstaff. Walter G. Walt for short." He stuck out his right hand.

Indiw took the hand in his own right, trying not to flinch at the touch of moist skin. This one was pale-colored with brown hair and eyes and sharp features. "You are the one whose partner died yesterday?"

"Uh—"

The human let go of Indiw's hand. His mouth tightened, and one hand made a fighting fist on the chair arm between them as if restraining the urge to hit Indiw.

I've done it again. "I shouldn't have said that. I apologize. There is emotional bonding between human flying partners. I will learn to think of these things before I speak." For the thousandth time in the last day, Indiw wished he'd paid better attention to the texts on human nature. But who could have predicted he'd need them?

"It's okay," grunted Falstaff, waving a hand.

"No, it is not." The carrier *Tacoma* had picked Indiw up in his one-seat fighter after the same battle in which Falstaff had lost his partner, the battle in which Indiw's carrier *Katukin*—manned exclusively by Ardr—had been destroyed. Indiw and three other Ardr—now in the humans' sickbay—had been the only survivors. "I have chosen to fight with you. This is your unit. Your rules apply. Insults, even unintentional ones, are not acceptable. I apologize."

Falstaff cocked his head to one side. "All right. Apology accepted. You any good as a pilot?"

"The best." He added modestly, "Among Ardr, that is."

"What should I call you?"

Indiw's hand flew to his vest where his name and rank were stitched in the symbols common to the three species of the First Tier, the alliance that had kept the peace in this part of the galaxy for nearly a century. "Indiw. Is it not clearly written?"

"Is that all? Just Indoo?"

"Indiyou," he tried more clearly. He wasn't about to explain it was an acrostic derived from some of the names he had earned through his short life. "Indiw is all you need to find my records."

"I just wanted to know what to call you—other than Pit Bull Four."

"Pit Bull Four?"

"Your call. We're Pit Bull. Grummon is our flight leader, so he's Pit Bull One. I'm Three. You're Four."

"Oh, code identification." He studied the stylized image on Falstaff's squadron patch. A bull? He was taken with a panicky revulsion he was hard put to mask. "Isn't a bull a male herd beast used to breed domesticated eating flesh?"

The human mouth opened, framed by the strip of hair and displaying perfect white teeth, good biting and tearing teeth— in front anyway. "Uh-yeeaahh," drawled Falstaff, "but a *pit* bull is a small, ferocious, sometimes vicious defender of its territory. A dog. They're so vicious it took two hundred years to breed judgment into the pit bull, but now they're the best security money and love can buy."

"I—see."

Falstaff sat back, nodding and smiling.

Dogs hunted in packs under a pack leader. In the early decades of the alliance with the humans, Ardr had made a detailed study of evolution on the humans' homeworld, searching for the basic essence of human nature in order to understand what they'd evolved into. Today, every Ardr learned how all the successful species on Earth ran in packs or herds or tribes ruled by a pack leader of some sort. Humans considered themselves The Human Family, and some of their cultures thought of themselves as their brothers' keepers and kept meddling in the affairs of other packs or groups of humans.

Species of lone hunters who held their territory singly had been exterminated by humans. The pack and herd creatures had been domesticated. And what was worse, the humans knew that Ardr had evolved from lone hunters forced to develop intelligence and civilization by the rise of pack hunters not too different from humans, though lacking intelligence.

It was oversimplified, perhaps, but too chillingly true, Indiw saw now. *Pit Bull Four.* What a symbol. He wanted to run from the room and never see another human again as long as he lived. But he had announced his choice.

"Commander Falstaff, before I make another grave error, may I ask you a delicate question?"

"Sure. Fire away."

Pleased that he knew the idiom, Indiw asked, "Pilot Commander Chancy—will she try to kill me today? Or will she wait until—"

"What?!"

"Pilot Commander Chancy—" Indiw started to repeat.

"No, I heard you. That's very perceptive actually. If I didn't know Marla so well, I wouldn't have known she was steamed about the deal. Look, Indiw, she's been bucking for a slot with Pit Bull ever since we won our third Flying Ace. We're the best squadron on *Tacoma,* and she's without doubt one of the top ten pilots aboard.

"If I know her—and I *do*—she's out in the hall right now scheming about ways to replace you. But she's not allowed to lay a finger on you—physically. It's a court-martial offense to attack a fellow officer—except on the sparring mats, properly clothed and under supervision. Do you understand? She's probably figuring out ways to get you back to your own people because that's the fastest way to get your slot."

"I—see." He digested that, grateful to the man for the frank explanation. "And you. Would you not prefer such a proven flyer off your wing?"

Falstaff's face changed in an intriguing way. Indiw wished mightily he'd worked with the videos on human expressions more. "Actually, Indiw, I'm not really sure that I would. Oh, she's good, all right. But—well—it's personal."

"Apologies." He sketched a conciliatory gesture, not at all sure the human could read it. But he knew no standard phrase to convey what he meant. Sexual innuendo couldn't be translated, and he was certain he'd trespassed in that delicate area.

"TEN—hut!" All the clamoring humans leapt to their feet, braced in that unnatural posture again, utterly silent, facing front.

Falstaff reached back and grabbed a handful of Indiw's flight suit, forcing him to his feet. "*Tacoma*'s Captain!"

The human hand was gone as quickly as it had fastened on him or the man might have lost it to Ardr teeth and claws. Quelling that instinctive reaction, Indiw pulled his feet together and tried to imitate the others. He felt ridiculous.

A man in a white shipboard uniform strode up the center aisle, his steps all the same size, his arms moving with his stride. He reached the front, turned, surveyed them as if memorizing their faces, then snapped, "Officers, be seated."

He was clean-shaven, and had even cleaned most of the hair off the top of his head. Even without horns, it was an improvement.

While Indiw was studying the ship's Captain, everyone around him bent down to sit leaving Indiw towering alone among them. Falstaff pulled him backward and he fell into his chair. There wasn't a sound in the room except the little catches in the breathing of the humans nearest Indiw.

The Captain paced the length of the platform to stand in front of the Pit Bull group. He looked them over. Even the breathing stopped. "Commander Indiyou. Welcome to the *Tacoma* and to Hundred Twentieth Fighter Wing. If you should experience any difficulties, be sure to call on me."

This, too, had to be part of their pack-forming liturgy, but he couldn't make out what it might really mean.

Indiw barely followed the introduction of the briefing, puzzling over Captain Sutcliff's words. But then the Captain brought up a familiar star map of the area on the big screen, a view of the border between the Tier worlds and the Hyos Empire.

"Here, here, and here, the Hyos have warned us—a day and a half late—of impending swarms. The Fornak are taking care of this region, and the Ardr have this under control. The first breakout occurred yesterday in the region *Tacoma* is supposed to keep clean. We lost the *Katukin* yesterday because we couldn't get here in time. Now the Ardr carrier *Katular* will have to cover its own and half of *Katukin*'s territory. So we must make short work of this job and move here to cover the other half of *Katukin*'s assigned area. Between the two carriers, we can hold all three territories until the Fornak can get their carrier into position to replace *Katukin*—at least until the Ardr can bring up another of theirs.

"I don't have to tell you what a politically ticklish situation this could become. The First Tier alliance is based on the principle that each of the three species will defend the territory of the others from aggressors—in this case the Hyos swarms. It is imperative that we not allow any Ardr world to be reached by a Hyos swarm, and this entire ship is committed to that objective. Is that understood? Any questions?"

Dead silence.

Indiw wondered if *Tacoma*'s Captain was performing specifically for his benefit, but since the humans seemed to ignore the call for questions, Indiw decided to keep silent as well. He obviously had a lot to learn about briefing liturgies.

Sutcliff clicked the viewscreen to a close-up of the Hyos border showing the segment the *Tacoma* usually patrolled with the additional part of *Katukin*'s territory *Tacoma* must now cover clearly marked.

The Hyos, having evolved from hive dwellers, had peculiar notions about territory. They didn't consider the taking of an inhabited world an invasion—or even an act of war. It was an act of reproduction to which no sane group could possibly object. With affable good humor, the Hyos warned the Tier when one of the Hyos worlds was about to send out a swarm. They were perfectly pleased to have the Tier destroy those swarms and thus maintain the current border. No Hyos world would, however, make any effort to restrain the swarms or direct them elsewhere.

" . . . so your job is to blast this swarm before it gets off the ground. The Hyos have given us the ground targeting data. If you hit anything outside that target area, it *could* lead to real war with the Hyos, so I want every one of you to triple check every bit of equipment and programming in your targeting systems. We can't afford trouble with the Hyos while our picket line is spread so thin. So there *will be no errors*—understood?"

"Yes, sir!" the humans chorused in one voice.

"Questions?"

A human voice, higher-pitched like Chancy's, asked, "Sir. Have the Hyos also warned the swarm that we're coming? And what our strike zone must be?"

"As always, we must assume so. It is the usual pattern along this stretch of border. You must be prepared for surprises."

Heads turned as glances were exchanged, but there were no other questions or comments as the computer fed each chair-arm desk station the data the pilots would need.

The Captain finished, "Keep in mind that this is not a unique situation. The Hyos have given us onworld targets before. Sometimes we obliterate the target and that's the end of it. But sometimes we don't get it all and they still swarm later. We can't afford that here. Because we've lost the *Katukin,* we have to get *all* of this swarm on first strike. There are three other swarms expected to try soon either for the Ardr world Sinaha or perhaps for our own Aberdeen.

"We've been given worlds of origin of those three swarms, two *very* crowded Hyos worlds. We haven't yet been invited to strike there on the ground. If there's any collateral damage from our strikes today, you can be sure we won't be given a chance at those nests situated in heavily populated areas. We'll have to fight those swarms here in Tier space, and it will be vicious. So we can't afford to lose anyone on this strike, and we can't afford any mistakes. Questions?"

Silence. It hadn't sounded like any sort of normal invitation to debate tactics, so Indiw kept silent, too. He hadn't learned anything. Except for the human liturgies, the entire "briefing" was an exercise in wasting time.

"Ten-hut! Dismiss!"

Everyone scrambled to their feet, grabbing the data cartridges out of their desk displays, and came to attention. Indiw clumsily followed suit. But before he achieved the braced stance, they broke ranks and human throats opened emitting a wash of sound that may have formed words but carried an undertow of cheerful threat couched in vaguely sexual terms. Some made mock aggressive moves at their compatriots as they retrieved their helmets.

The sight made Indiw's skin tighten and his gorge rise. How could he fly with undisciplined children? But of course, these weren't Ardr children mocking adult combat. These were humans performing some arcane public ritual for bonding themselves into a hunting pack. It would have been mildly interesting if he hadn't committed himself to become a part of it, if only for a while.

He secured his helmet and tucked his briefing cartridge into his belt.

A heavy hand clapped down on his shoulder and he spun, dropping away from the touch into fighting stance, claws out, teeth bared. He was facing Falstaff.

The human froze, eyes wide enough to expose white above the colored area. He backed off, clumsily imitating the proper placating move.

Barely in time, Indiw aborted the trained move and straightened, forcibly quelling the rush. Noticing their flight leader was watching, he said softly, "Don't ever do that, Falstaff. *Never.*"

"Sorry. I forgot."

Indiw answered by imitating Falstaff's own hand-waving gesture. "It's okay. You startled me, that's all."

"It is not all right," said Falstaff in a chiding imitation of Indiw's own words as he began to move toward the door. "They make us take classes in alien customs all the time, to be sure we don't do something dumb like that. I only meant to be friendly."

"So I gathered. *After* I almost killed you."

Falstaff paused, pulling Indiw aside with a gesture carefully made in midair. "Listen. I'll give you the best advice I got when I reported for pilot's training. It's the one clue you need in order to fit in around here, and with that, you'll be okay."

"I'm listening."

"Don't volunteer. Never—ever—volunteer. Just fade back into the crowd and be as inconspicuous as you can."

Nothing Falstaff could have said would have made Indiw feel more alien among these people. The best advice they had for a new pilot was to become one of the pack. He shuddered.

Falstaff nodded happily and headed for the door again, shuffling behind the crowd. The Pit Bull flight leader, Grummon, caught up with them. "Case of nerves, Indoo?"

Indiw tensed against the insult. He'd promised himself he'd do all the proper respect formulas. He'd refreshed his memory on the sigils that indicated rank, and he'd memorized where they'd placed him in their hierarchy, so he'd get the formulas correct. His mind was so stuffed with alien trivia crammed in during the last few hours that he barely knew what he knew. He'd gone to so much trouble to be allowed to fly, he mustn't gut his flight leader before they'd even made greeting. He looked at the man. *Maybe afterward, though.*

"That was my fault, sir," Falstaff interrupted. "I forgot you're not supposed to touch an Ardr from behind. Indiyou's not nervous. He's ready to get the bastards that got his buddies. Right?"

Indiw dredged a memory from his studies and made reverence to the flight leader with the hand salute to superiors, trying to copy Chancy's crisp execution of it. "Sir, Pilot Commander Indiw reporting for duty. Sir!"

"At ease, Commander. We're an informal squadron. You keep your place and do what you're told, we'll be back in time for dinner. You *can* fly formation, can't you? I mean even though the Ardr don't fight in formation?"

"Yes, sir." This morning he'd also reviewed the fighting formations used by the humans. They were easy enough to fly. It just seemed like such a tactically stupid thing to do. Nevertheless, humans who'd perfected it were deadly adversaries. The trick was to make sure every single craft was in its correct spot in their rigid pattern. "No problem, sir."

"Then just be sure that no matter what, you stay with Falstaff here. You guard his back, let him take the target out. Got that?"

"Yes, sir!"

Grummon nodded, then marched out and disappeared into the sea of identical backs in the hall. Falstaff said, "Don't let him get to you. He didn't mean to treat you like a rookie. . . ."

Falstaff went on while Indiw groped for the idiom, found it, and decided that that was exactly what Grummon had meant to do. A man that offensive wouldn't have lived ten minutes on *Katukin.* By the time Indiw picked up the thread of Falstaff's comments, they were out in the passage, following the crowd to the launch bay.

" . . . so this squadron has an ancient and honored history. Just remember you're Pit Bull Four, and your job is to get my ordnance load to target. Got that?"

"Got it," he said, forcing himself to add, "Pit Bull Three."

"Good. See you out there—Pit Bull Four." The human fist didn't quite make contact with Indiw's shoulder. Maybe he could get to like this Falstaff.

"Walt!"

Falstaff's head snapped aside and he peeled off to work his way to the edge of the moving stream of people. Indiw hung back to see what the problem was, and only then realized that "Walt" was another of Falstaff's names—called in Chancy's voice.

Without Falstaff by his side, the crowd closed in about him and jostled and crushed him. He staggered to the bulkhead and clung there, letting the pilots stream by as he fought down the urge to attack. *Loathsome creatures!*

By the time he'd got hold of himself again and rejoined the press, it was less crushing. And he found himself just a step behind Falstaff and Chancy, close enough to hear them when nobody else could.

"Listen, Marla, it's not the end of the world. He won't be here long. He doesn't like it here any better than you'd like it on an Ardr ship."

"That's part of what worries me. He's going to screw you and leave you high and dry with enemy coming from every direction. An Ardr just isn't a team player, Walt."

Falstaff's arm snaked around her very small waist and he snugged her close to him. Their steps matched perfectly even though she was shorter. "You wouldn't trust my back to anyone but you."

She squirmed away. "Not in the hall! If word gets around that we're sleeping together, we'll never get to fly together. You know policy!"

Now that's one strange policy! And then Indiw thought again, and remembered that "*sleeping together*" didn't mean *sleeping* at all. It was an idiom like "going for a walk." But that made it an even stranger policy. How could the one thing interfere with the other?

Indiw preferred to attract the females in his own wing. It provided a deeper understanding of a person's temperament, and that always helped—or maybe it wouldn't if you had to fly in a rigid formation? And then he remembered humans often used sexual behaviors as another pack or even exclusive pair bonding ritual. Now *that* could cause problems in combat if two females broke formation to fight each other over a male.

"You," said Falstaff, picking up the pace, "are the one who has to be careful. S&R's not the safest assignment in the fleet either, you know. I'll be back for dinner, and we'll crack a magnum together, okay?"

She shook her head in the negation gesture. "On S&R, I'll hardly ever be here when you're here! Besides, tonight I have to sit on the Croninwet Committee. We need to get the recommendations to Aberdeen in a few days where the awards decisions will be made."

"Well, maybe we'll meet in the big Out There!"

She punched his arm. "Don't even *say* things like that!"

"You know I'm invincible!"

"The hell you are! You're just the luckiest pilot in the wing!"

"*Lucky!* My lady, that is not luck, that is skill!"

"Skill my big toe! You fly like a fat lizard! If I were on your wing, I'd have to spend all my time nursemaiding you! The Hyos would *laugh* themselves helpless!"

"Marla!" he reproached her. "We're the two best pilots in the wing. Less than a tenth of a point separates us in the ratings, and I'll beat you next time!"

"How much would you bet?"

"A month's pay!"

"Two."

"Done."

She pulled away as they reached the entrance to the flight deck. "Walt—shit, man, despite your insane reliance on luck, you are the only real pilot among these amateurs. I *want* to fly with you—for the sheer sensuous joy of it, if nothing else!"

"Don't worry. Now I have to come back. Gotta collect on that bet."

"We'll just see who's doing the collecting." She turned away, then checked, grabbing Falstaff's arm. "Don't be a hero. Just do your job and come back." She hit him on the arm again in a way that solidly confirmed their thwarted sexual arousal, and then she was gone.

Don't be a hero? What a very odd thing for a *human* to say in a parting admonition. Surely it had to be an idiom.

Indiw followed Falstaff onto the flight deck and on into the echoing launch bay with the weird feeling he'd just barged in on somebody else's walk. He kept expecting Falstaff to turn and try to gut him, which was irrational. Falstaff had done and said those things in full public view. The texts all warned there was no limit to what some humans would do in public, while others were more reticent.

Without the least hint of disturbance at what Indiw might have overheard, Falstaff fell back beside Indiw and pointed out the Ardr fighter on the line. Perhaps he was the unlimited type. In that case, it was a very, *very* good thing Falstaff wasn't trapped on an Ardr ship with a human female companion.

Engineers were still working on some of the battle-scarred craft. It was obvious how much it had cost *Tacoma* to try to save *Katukin*. It was impressive, but the motive behind their all-out effort was a mystery to Indiw. In like circumstance, *Katukin* would have withdrawn to waylay the enemy while they celebrated their victory, and he was sure *Tacoma*'s Captain Sutcliff knew that.

As it was, the effort to save *Katukin* had allowed several swarm ships to get past them. It was still an open question whether the swarm's Breeder had been on one of those ships and whether other ships would be able to intercept before they reached the planet they'd been heading toward. He thought that might well be Aberdeen.

He found his own craft unrecognizable under a coat of paint, sporting the Pit Bull Squadron's symbols and a large 4 under the insignia of *Tacoma*. At least they'd left the original First Tier chevrons in place.

He climbed into the familiar cockpit, trying not to notice the exterior. At least the worn seat still conformed to his back, and the controls adjusted readily to comfort level. And all the damage had been competently repaired.

At a touch, the displays came up bright and clear, and when he inserted the briefing cartridge, the data came up in the format he was used to. He set the fighter's own diagnostic routines to running, and then concentrated on absorbing an overview of the tactical situation.

He found the nearest Ardr carrier, *Katular,* moving in to cover part of *Katukin*'s territory, while *Tacoma* covered the rest. He charted their relative positions by time, and then expanded the view to show the border and the Hyos worlds beyond.

But when he asked for the global tactical situation, his map became overlaid with just a few lines and symbols.

He'd expected that, but he still had to choke back indignation. He was only a pilot. Here he wasn't entitled to all the information the carrier's top decision makers had. Here, only a few people knew enough about what was happening to make decisions, and everyone else just carried out those decisions, having no way to decide for themselves whether they wanted to do what was suggested or not. Even though the very idea turned his bone marrow to water, he had to accept that if he wanted to fly.

And I do want to fly.

On Sinaha, one of the Ardr worlds behind the line they were defending, there was a nice wooded range that would be his own someday—if the Hyos didn't get it first.

He pulled his light translating goggles down around his neck and brought up a picture of it, so he could retune his display to the correct colors from his real memory of the place.

The screen showed a clear stream burbling over glistening white rocks, green shrubbery, tall trees arching over the stream. Where one had fallen, a shaft of misty sunlight illuminated a flower-strewn clearing where, one day, he'd build his dwelling. His service as a pilot had already earned him forty percent of the monetary price and was well on the way to satisfying the other requirements.

He could smell the tree sap, hear the wildlife, feel the silken wind. Suddenly he ached to hunt.

"Home?" A human voice. Falstaff's voice.

The human was standing on the scaffold looking into the cockpit over Indiw's shoulder. Reorienting with an effort, Indiw translated the question. "Yes, I guess you'd say so." Smoothly he replaced the image with the tactical diagrams that now showed up in perfect color ratios.

"Looks really nice."

"Yes, your engineers did a fine job on the burned circuits, and now the color's tuned, the data display is perfect." He wondered what the color looked like to the human eye. He replaced his goggles and could barely make out the display lines.

Falstaff said, "I just wanted to make sure you'd understood all the targeting specifics and had done your triple checks on your systems. Your fighter was pretty badly torn up when we got you aboard yesterday."

"Diagnostics check out perfectly," Indiw answered stiffly, remembering Chancy's opinion of him as a flying partner. Falstaff, no doubt, agreed, no matter what he'd told her. But the man had chosen to come in person rather than use the com and let everyone know that he didn't trust his new wingman. "Now that I've got the displays tuned, I was going to check the mechanics directly. Want to help? Then I'll help you."

"Well, we don't usually— Is that an Ardr procedure?"

"No—it's a *Katukin* custom. Four eyes may see what two eyes miss. We had a well-earned reputation."

"Okay." He grinned. "Let's do it *Katukin* style."

Indiw grabbed a probe, and climbed out of the cockpit. He thought he sensed a strain in Falstaff, as if he was trying hard to overcome his distrust, or perhaps just trying to establish a bond that Indiw kept unconsciously rejecting. Considering that his former wingman had let him down, and he'd just been robbed of the one pilot in the wing who could out-fly him, the human was being very brave.

As they opened hatches, attached leads, and squinted at readouts, and did it all over again on Falstaff's fighter, Indiw made a conscious effort to communicate his trustworthiness to the human. Even when their hands accidentally knocked into each other, he didn't let his claws extend. Much.

If the human's nerve failed because he didn't trust Indiw, they could both be killed, and that could leave a hole in the formation that might cause the whole attack to fail. It might be a stupid way to conduct a combat mission, but it was the way they did things here. And when they did it right, they were at least as good as any Ardr battle group.

So as they worked, Indiw discussed every detail of the briefing data they'd allowed him to see, all the targeting data, and every possible variation of the action he could envision. About halfway through his recital, Falstaff began to open up, and they exchanged anecdotes of other onworld targets they'd attacked.

They finished checking the heavy missiles slung under Falstaff's fighter where Indiw carried smaller, lighter ordnance destined for moving targets. Falstaff gave one of the weapons an affectionate pat. "If it comes to a dogfight, just remember, you stick right there"—he pointed to a spot behind and above one wing—"and watch out behind us. Until I get rid of this stuff, I'll wallow like a pregnant cow."

So, the human hadn't understood a word Indiw had said.

Stiffly Indiw replied, "I understand my duties. I understand that if we each do our job, the entire operation will succeed. I will do my job."

"Of—" started Falstaff. He sighed, rubbed the back of his neck, then looked Indiw in the eyes. "I'll be counting on you. Let's go!"

Moments later Falstaff climbed into his cockpit, closed his canopy over his head, and brought his fighter up to readiness for launch.

Indiw scrambled to his own cockpit and secured for launch. His com had been retuned to get the humans on his primary channel, Ardr on two, with the Fornak frequency on three. He could monitor all three simultaneously if he needed to. Now, Pit Bull One was chanting them through another liturgy, this one disguised as a preflight check and countdown.

Indiw answered with the prescribed monosyllables and shunted his opinion of it all to one side. Now he had a mission to fly. Later, he could think.

★
CHAPTER
TWO
★

TACOMA'S LAUNCH PROCESS WAS NEARLY IDENTICAL TO *Katukin*'s, as all Tier engineering was fully compatible. Here the lighting was a little different, but the com chatter still had the feel of a group of people familiar with each other going out to do a routine job. *When the objective is to live through it all, it can't really be so different. Can it?*

Tacoma Launch Control pulled his fighter into the launch tube, lined it up, then turned the controls over to him. Indiw shot himself out of the launch tube right behind Pit Bull Three, and in one neat move fell into the position Falstaff had specified.

He got the acknowledgment from Falstaff he wanted and quietly made a rude gesture toward Pit Bull One. *Nerves! Ha!*

The squadron pulled together and waited as the wing's formation assembled around them. Pit Bull was in the middle of the pack with three other squadrons carrying heavy ordnance. The rest were there to protect them and deliver them to target—and maybe home again, too. Maybe.

"Pit Bull Four, this is Red Leader. Acknowledge." It was a deep, resonant voice that came across very clearly.

"Pit Bull Four acknowledging Red Leader," said Indiw.

"Pit Bull Four, you do know my commands override even Pit Bull One's?"

"Yes, sir, Red Leader."

There was a very faint chorus of laughter, hardly more than a few grunts and chuckles.

"Pit Bull Four, that's yes, ma'am, Red Leader," corrected the voice that was in command of the entire pack.

"Sorry. Yes, ma'am, Red Leader." Red was the name of the color of human blood. An appropriate squadron name.

"You will recognize my voice now?"

"Yes, ma'am, Red Leader."

Red Leader issued terse instructions, and the pack—*wing,* he corrected himself—settled down for the four-hour run to target. Even at two lights, it would take that long.

Indiw spent the time studying the targeting data and attack plan. But there was so little available to him that it made him feel like a helpless victim not a fighter pilot protecting his territory. In desperation, he focused his attention on the humans doing their bonding liturgies in profane and sexual tones. He couldn't imagine what it must be like to have one's sexuality all bound up in one's aggressive/defensive instincts. *Talk about evolution handing out a raw deal!*

When they were in range of the border with Hyos territory, they dropped below lightspeed to take their bearings. These small craft couldn't carry the gear for long-range astrogation.

With course corrections laid in, they went silent, engaged their stealth shielding, and separated to scatter any leakage they might be trailing. Red Leader's last order was "Pit Bull Four, you be sure to stick with Pit Bull Three."

"Yes, ma'am, Red Leader." How many times were they going to tell him? He had chosen this after all. But then every instructor on alien behavior warned not to expect decency from other species. He supposed the humans had been similarly warned and didn't expect him to display ordinary human decency. That was probably wise advice.

Before they'd penetrated far beyond the border zone, a few Hyos tracings flared across the scopes, distant ships going about their business. The established Hyos rarely helped a swarm by warning of incoming attacks, though they would let the swarm know they'd been targeted. But by the same token, they wouldn't help the attackers, either, except to locate the swarm's nest and grant permission to pulverize it. After it declared itself, the swarm's fate was no longer a matter of interest to the Hyos establishment.

But a swarm wasn't an unintelligent foe. The swarm consisted of young Hyos, well educated, well trained, talented in every way Hyos could be, easily the equal of any species of the First Tier. They had spaceships, and colonizing equipment, offensive and defensive armament, and all the training and—unlike their settled relatives—the will to use their training to take territory.

The target world loomed in the scopes, showing swirling clouds, sparkling oceans, and teaming cities sprawling across the land masses. While they were still far out in space, Indiw's targeting systems pinpointed the swarm's installation in a high mountain valley far from anything else.

He studied the energy use patterns, life signs, metallic masses that had to be ships. Much of the complex might be underground, but still—there wasn't enough metal there. But there was no time to think. They were already skimming the outermost radiation belts just above the atmosphere.

"This is Red Leader. Deploy for atmosphere. Orbiters, take position."

The fighters deployed their stubby wings for the steep glide in. Pit Bull came down in formation, Indiw right where Falstaff wanted him to be, already watching their rear habitually.

It was a textbook perfect attack run. Despite the clouds, the missiles slid neatly into their trajectories, acquired their targets, and began evasive maneuvers before any return fire came up from the ground. Falstaff's missiles burrowed deep into the underground complex in concert with those laid by the other squadrons, and on cue, the surface heaved and fell in, forming a deep pit.

Still, return fire came up at them, hot and heavy. It hit when the attackers were at the bottom of their descent, fighting gravity and air, craft straining and shaking to pull up. Just the sound wave they were leaving behind them was enough to destroy buildings.

The squadrons carrying lighter ordnance dove deeper, strafing the surface complex and its low altitude defenses. Even so, Pit Bull fighters were buffeted by wild energies from the densely placed surface weapons. Explosions kicked him out of his slot and he had to fight his computer, overriding the safeties to keep him in position. He hated atmosphere flying.

Then Pit Bull One called orders and the squadron recovered, and swept around back into the formation and returned on target. This time, it was Indiw's turn to ride down in front with Falstaff behind him, for Indiw was carrying the slender pinpoint-accurate missiles to take out ground weaponry.

Pit Bull One assigned him the installation atop a stone outcropping, above the swarm's hangars. Rows of big transports sat on the field before the hangars, but there were few fighters down there. No tankers. That was all he had time to note.

He found his target, a defensive gun that threw a spinning shaft of energy that could slice up a fighter. Suddenly things seemed familiar. *This* he'd done dozens of times before, and he knew just how to go about it.

He brought up the standard subroutines he needed, input the data, set up the attack run, and rode the ship down in its steepest power dive, ten percent beyond specs but still safer than getting sliced up. The program released his preprimed missile when he was so close, going so fast, that the slicer couldn't respond. Then he penetrated the slicer's cone of effectiveness and right over the center of his target installation, his program pulled him up from the dive, mashing him helplessly into his seat.

He was gone before the stationary installations defending his target could track, lock on, and destroy him.

When the explosion bloomed behind him, kicking him hard, he was lying on his back, his fighter in a vertical climb, taking advantage of the extra push from the explosion to pile on the gravities. Four agonizing breaths later, the force let up enough for him to report, "Pit Bull One, I got the slicer."

"Pit Bull Four, what the hell kinda damnfool stunt was that? This is a squadron not a circus! And prepriming is against regs! G'dammit, where's Falstaff?"

Indiw had forgotten all about the human. He suddenly remembered that most humans couldn't make the stress tolerances that some Ardr could, and he was top in stress tolerance among Ardr. Had Falstaff tried that climb and blacked out? But no, there he was in the scope, approaching from the rear, closing back into position.

"I'm here, Grummon. Helluva ride, but I killed a fighter that came within a hair of getting Pit Bull Four."

"But—!" Indiw cut off his objection. He had seen nothing. He said, "Pit Bull Three, thank you."

"Day's work," replied Falstaff. "And it's not over yet. Just don't pull any more shit, okay?"

The flight leader had marshaled the squadron into formation with the other squadrons that had gone down. Before Indiw had a chance to verify for himself that they'd cleared the entire target area, they were driving for orbit, exchanging routine commentary on the swarm's response. Though the ground-based fire had been heavier than anyone had ever seen before, there had been few fighters rising to greet them. They had lost no craft, though some were damaged.

Indiw cut across the self-congratulatory chatter to say, "Check out the metallic mass readings down there, then the ratio of transports to fighters. There are lots of fighters missing."

Red Leader and the flight leaders conferred while the attackers rejoined the orbiters and took turns refueling for the trip home, which would take longer. *Tacoma* was already far from where they had left it, and would be farther still by the time they rendezvoused.

Orbital observations showed no activity around the swarm's installation. The humans in authority concluded the missing fighters just hadn't been built yet. They'd killed the target. When Indiw objected, Grummon cut off his com link to the rest of the wing and told him in a growling tone, "We got the Breeder. Couple dozen fighters don't matter. The swarm is killed. I don't want to hear your voice again!"

The com clicked and chuckled, and the chatter resumed. Then Indiw was too busy to pay attention as he nuzzled up to the tanker and refueled. His steep vertical climb had used up a prodigious amount of fuel, and so when they pulled the plug on him, his gauges showed not quite full. Still, it should get him back to *Tacoma*.

While his fighter was drinking the hyperpressed matter/antimatter powder from the tanker, and afterward, as he stood off to guard during Falstaff's refueling, he scanned for Hyos craft. There was a lot of traffic in orbit, but no formations of tiny masses bristling with energy. As the pack re-formed for the jump past light speed, Indiw engaged one of his own surveillance programs. Instead of focusing on the rear, as Falstaff had instructed him, he let the program scan globally with maximum sensitivity forward along their course home.

That sensitivity caused every little blip to set off his alarms, which made him flex his claws. He knew there had to be swarm fighters hunting them but the humans didn't believe in them because their *leaders* told them not to. He wanted to set his own course back to *Tacoma,* not sit here as part of a huge, obvious target.

If they really had gotten the Breeder, those fighters had nothing to live for. If they hadn't, the swarm fighters would be determined to open a hole in the Tier defense line. Either way, those missing Hyos fighters were a menace it was pointless to face with such reduced ammunition.

Nearing the border with Tier space, Red Leader gave the order to drop below lightspeed for course correction. And it was a good thing, too, because they were much farther from the border than their instruments had indicated. In fact, they were still deep in enemy territory.

Indiw tensed, eyes flicking over his displays. He was the first to spot them.

"Incoming, dead astern!" he warned, despite Pit Bull One's injunction against his voice being heard on the com again. "Fifteen blips." There had to be more somewhere.

Another voice reported thirty more sightings, but cut off in midword. "This is Silver Wolf Two. Silver Wolf One's gone. Form on me, Silver Wolves." Another voice cut in reporting an uncounted number of Hyos closing fast.

Red Leader murmured orders in cold, cool tones. Grummon's voice blurred across her words. Falstaff answered for Pit Bull Three and Four, and suddenly they were very busy. Indiw had thought he understood human space battle formations from reading and simulator practice, and perhaps he did in theory, but the reality was something else.

The next long minutes were a blur of stretching tension followed by blazing action. Indiw never did gain a grasp of the battle as a whole, never did reach the point of confidence he was accustomed to in the heat of combat. He followed Falstaff through the maneuvers, half his mind concentrating on understanding what the human was doing, trying to anticipate his next move. The other half tracked the Hyos by sheer habit.

Three times, Hyos craft vanished in the blaze of his weapons, and two more times he sliced pieces off enemies. Neutralized, the humans would say. Once Grummon took out a Hyos missile Indiw had been unable to shake. Falstaff killed two enemy craft, but he missed one that went on to collide with Red Leader. Bits of debris pinged against Indiw's craft, penetrating his now tattered energy shields.

In panic, he wondered what the humans would do now their leader was slain, but another voice took over command of the battle as smoothly and coolly as the woman's had. *Of course, chain of command.* They never ran out of leaders until the last human was dead. Why had he forgotten that?

Falstaff dove into the thick of the swarm fighters, and Indiw was too busy to think. His job was to stay with Falstaff and guard his back. And he did his job. He lost count of how many times flame blossomed at the far reach of his weapons. Once, he flew directly at a Hyos bearing down on Falstaff, and forced the other to change course. Then he got him on a softened rear shield. The Hyos vaporized, and Indiw circled back to chase Falstaff into another knot of Hyos.

Somewhere on the periphery of his awareness, the rest of Pit Bull harried the same group of fighters he and Falstaff were nibbling on. It was like a tightly choreographed mating dance, but he had to keep looking at everyone else's feet to see what he was supposed to be doing.

He took some more impact damage from debris, but it was minor. The sleeting radiation was worse. Where a shield had softened for a moment, radiation seared one of his weapons' control circuits. He went to backup, but it was sluggish. Nobody else was unscathed. Even Grummon's craft showed scorch marks.

A nearby blast whited out all his screens, and for three heart-stopping seconds, he flew blind, fighting to align his shields against the barrage. He came out the other side, and his canopy, momentarily robbed of its energy sheath, was suddenly coated with the infinitely dangerous granules of fighter fuel. His scope showed him Falstaff's craft, just ahead of him, holed and leaking. "Pit Bull Three, you're spewing fuel. Shut down!"

"Can't. Stay with me, Indiw." And they were around and driving toward a Hyos that was chasing Grummon. Grummon's wingman was engaged with two other Hyos while Grummon dodged a missile and tried to fry its brain with a scramble beam.

Indiw had no time to vibrate his shields and carefully shake that stuff off his canopy. Jaw clenched, eyes closed, he just rammed the shield back to full power. When he knew he'd survived, he looked, and sure enough, the granules were gone.

But there was a Hyos on his tail. He fired just as the Hyos entered the cloud of fuel Indiw had shed.

The Hyos and the fuel went up in a spectacular ball of fire. Hard radiation sleeted through everything.

Falstaff went for the Hyos on Grummon's tail. That Hyos broke off, turned, and came after Indiw. Indiw twisted, dove, and climbed in the maneuver prescribed for giving Falstaff a clean shot at the Hyos. His craft screamed its protest, circuits crackled, and the fire controls triggered behind his cockpit somewhere. Everything on his boards was redlined. He shut off the audio alarms.

To Indiw's utter surprise, the maneuver worked. Falstaff whooped his triumph a split instant before the Hyos blew apart, but the whoop turned to a roar of surprise. When his screens cleared, Indiw saw the gaping hole in the starboard side of Falstaff's craft.

But his scanners were clear. There were no more Hyos. The only blips with Tier colors were the four of Pit Bull Squadron. Everything else was lifeless debris. Everything.

There was a silent interval of collecting their wits, and Indiw felt his own sense of completion. He'd done what he'd set out to do. He'd fought with the humans. They'd won. And he'd lived through it. Then Grummon's voice asked, "Any of you see any survivors?"

"Nothing here," reported Grummon's wingman grimly.

"My scans are a little hazy, but I don't see anything. Unless some of them took off, we're the only survivors."

"That's how I make it," agreed Grummon. "What about you, Pit Bull Four?"

"I show only debris and us four."

"Three," corrected Falstaff. "I'm totaled. I'm never going to make it back to *Tacoma*."

Indiw's first thought was of Falstaff's cocky promise to Marla Chancy, but he couldn't remind Falstaff of that over the open circuit. Grummon solved the problem human style. He ordered Falstaff into place in the formation and pointed them toward the border.

Limping along at Falstaff's best pace, they compared damage reports and exchanged astrogation data, checking each other's figures for radiation-induced errors. Nobody was getting really reliable answers, so they took an average. Then they estimated how close to *Tacoma* Falstaff might possibly get before he became inert debris. They chose a point where Falstaff could cut his drive and coast from there, conserving life support until his oxygen ran out.

"All right, that's it," said Grummon at last. "Falstaff, you stay on this course and conserve oxygen. We'll send S&R to pick you up."

"Make sure it's not Chancy. I don't like to be crowed over."

"My sympathies, but it'd be better than suffocating."

"Not by much."

As Indiw had suspected, human females could be as difficult to deal with as Ardr women.

"Come on, guys," said Pit Bull One, "we're still in Hyos space, and we've got a report to file." Grummon led off, increasing his speed as his wingman fell in beside him without comment.

Indiw didn't move from Falstaff's flank.

Grummon snapped, "Pit Bull Four, move it!"

"No, sir, I'm with Pit Bull Three, sir."

"Commander Indoo, get your ass up here. Now! That is an order."

Indiw didn't answer. He couldn't argue within their warped reasoning, but he knew what he had chosen to do, and he was going to do it.

Falstaff said, "Indiw, he has the right to give that order. You have to go."

"I'm staying." He'd heard Falstaff's voice in many tones now. He knew Falstaff was as astounded and outraged at Grummon's order as he himself felt.

"Look," said Falstaff, "there's no sense putting both of us at risk. They'll send S&R for me as soon as you get into com range of *Tacoma*. They'll be here before you've even finished debriefing."

"I'm staying."

"Indiw, there's nothing you can do for me—"

"I am staying."

Indiw himself wasn't sure why he was so firmly committed. But he had made his choice, and the more they tried to chivvy him out of it, the more offended he became. Could no one here respect the concept of choice?

Up ahead, Pit Bull One and his wingman were comparing notes on fuel and distance. Grummon said, "We've got to go or we'll never make it ourselves. Sit tight, Falstaff. Indiw, you are on report."

A flash of color, and the two fighters were gone, driving toward home at two lights.

"Falstaff? Is it very serious to be on report?"

"It can be. But in your case, somehow I don't think so."

"Because I was right?"

"God, no! Because you're Ardr. You fought so well, I think Grummon was just surprised you suddenly defied him."

"I wasn't defying him!"

"No? That should be an interesting one to hear. But we're not supposed to be talking. We're supposed to be conserving oxygen."

They fell silent and engaged the brain wave stimulator that would slow their metabolisms, keeping them alert to the alarms, yet relaxed. But Indiw's mind gnawed at his vitals. Staying had been a really stupid thing to do by anybody's measure. He couldn't explain it to the humans, and he'd *never* be able to explain it to his own people. Of course, *they* would just accept it as his choice. He hoped. But he did have to explain it to himself, and he didn't know how.

To stop his fruitless fretting, Indiw reconfigured his boards and recharted their course progress toward their rendezvous point using a different mathematics than the humans had used to strike their average. Then he added *Tacoma*'s ever shifting position.

It would be moving away from the rendezvous at considerable speed. Like all Ardr carriers, the human carrier *Tacoma* was the base for four complete fighter wings with all support vessels. The other wings would be flying other missions. *Tacoma* had to be in position to pick them up, too, or to support them if they came home trailing a swarm of Hyos fighters.

He tried to figure how soon Grummon would be in com range, and how soon *Tacoma* could dispatch a rescue, exactly when it could reach the rendezvous point where Falstaff would go inert. He checked his figures, then checked them again. The humans' average figures had been way off. No way could the pickup reach that rendezvous before Falstaff—and Indiw—ran out of air. Using Grummon's figures, they wouldn't even try.

He checked the calculations again, then checked his circuits. The formulas he was now using accessed a different processor than the one he'd used to help Grummon's calculations. This processor wasn't balky and weak. It hadn't been scrambled so badly by radiation. And even when he checked the math mentally, it came out the same. They weren't going to make it.

Falstaff was leaking fuel, and had almost lost superlight capability, probably from that second rent in his starboard side. Indiw's own craft was damaged as well, though he had fuel and power. Under strain, he might spring some seals or blow some circuits. No telling which ones. If he accelerated hard now to try to reach *Tacoma* and get help for Falstaff—he could very well find himself entombed in a helpless ship with no one knowing where to look for him.

He was pondering the options when a new cloud of vapor puffed out of the hole in Falstaff's craft. Simultaneously the com crackled with a loud noise, and the craft went sublight. Indiw tracked him down only because his instrument lock on Falstaff kicked him sublight, too. Even so, Indiw had to reduce his acceleration by half to stay with Falstaff.

"Pit Bull Three, what happened?" asked Indiw.

"Dunno. Wait—wait—ah, shit! The seal on my number two thruster went. That's it, Indiw. You better get out of here. I've been checking the calculations for hours, and there's still a chance you might make it."

So the human had been running the same calculations he had—and had been getting the same answer.

"Go on. What are you waiting for? You can still make it to *Tacoma*, but in a few minutes, that won't be possible. Tell them—"

"No!" He had an idea. He worked his screens as fast as he could, searching for the data he needed.

"Indiw, this is no time for—"

"No, listen! I've been running the calculation, too, assuming we *had* to make it back to *Tacoma*. But you see, *Tacoma* is moving away from us because *Katular* is moving *toward* us! *Katular* is moving into position to pick up one of its own battle groups that attacked another planet-bound swarm, don't you remember, it was in the morning briefing—"

"What are you talking about?"

He couldn't believe the humans didn't even read their own briefing materials. Maybe they only remembered what pertained to their own missions. But this was no time to—aha! "I've got it! *Katular*'s inside our range. If it's kept to its plan, it should be heading directly toward us now. But to make contact, we've got to turn. Here, look at this plot." He sent his map and tactical overlays to the human.

"Lord, I'd never make the turn. Indiw, I've only got one wheezing engine!"

"If we don't try it, we'll both die before *Tacoma* can find us. When they don't find us at rendezvous, they'll look along our plotted line of approach, but they'll expect we'll be traveling at the calculated velocity Grummon gave them. It'll be days, maybe weeks, till they find us—if they even keep looking after they know we're dead."

Falstaff thought about it for a while, and Indiw could hear the bleeps as he calculated. "In about two days, they'll turn the search over to *Katular*. You're right. They're much closer. But physics is the same in any culture. I still can't make the turn."

"Yes, you can!" As he said it, he knew how it could be done. "Your screens are intact. Mine are in bad shape, but my impulse cannon is functioning." *After a fashion.* He hadn't mentioned the sluggish response his backup circuits had been giving him at the end of the battle.

"What good is that?" asked the human.

But Indiw's hands were racing over his controls, modeling his idea and running simulations as he made adjustments. "We can do it. I know we can. We have to."

"G'dammit, man, what are you talking about!"

"All right, look at this!" He sent the simulation display over, and explained, "You turn off propulsion and power up your shields on just one side, and I power down my cannon. I come around to here, into just the right position, and I hit your shields with little punches, little taps, not too much in any one place to break through the shield. See, it *will* transfer momentum! You feel it when something hits your shields in battle. You'll feel it now. Only without propulsion to correct for it, you'll go where I send you."

"Good God!"

After he got over the shock of it, Falstaff argued. It was an insane plan. It couldn't be done.

Indiw, at his wit's end as the clock ate up the time, finally countered, "Well, if you don't try it, you'll surely never collect on that bet with Commander Chancy!"

There was a long, profound silence. Then Falstaff said, "That's a point." And after that he listened to Indiw's plans, at first leery, then awed, then enthusiastic.

Within fifteen minutes they had the thing set up. At first, Indiw had his cannon powered down too far. But little by little, they made the tricky adjustments. He was afraid he might miss the one stiffened shield and hit Falstaff. He was afraid his circuitry would malfunction and make the cannon emit a blast that would pulverize anything, shields or no. He was afraid the whole idea was as idiotic as it sounded. Mostly, he was just afraid.

But his hands were steady as he worked with his controls, and Falstaff's voice coached him in a low, calm tone that made the whole thing seem like a simulator exercise. After a while, he simply concentrated on perfecting the program he taught his system for the maneuver.

And then, unbelievably, they were around and onto the course they needed. Falstaff stiffened his rear shield instead of the flank, and Indiw repositioned. This time, Falstaff engaged his propulsion system at the same time. When Indiw was in position and matching his acceleration, they had to recompute the cannon shots and the shield power.

Falstaff, using most of his limited resources for his remaining engine, couldn't shield his rear as strongly as he'd shielded his flank.

Several times they had to stop when shielding wavered and let a blast through. Falstaff's craft couldn't take any more. Then they'd compute their E.T.A. against the remaining oxygen supply, and realize they *had* to keep at it. So once more they'd estimate how much the remaining shield could take and Indiw calibrated his cannon very carefully.

They worked up to a good clip, but it just wasn't enough. Perhaps if they'd started earlier, they might have made it. But as it was they'd be dead two hours before they reached *Katular*.

When Falstaff's shield finally did fail completely from the cannon barrage, *Katular* was still so far outside their com range that it was pointless to try, but Indiw set up the automatic distress call anyway.

"What are you doing?" asked Falstaff.

"Well, maybe someone will pick it up and relay it."

"Who? Hyos?"

"We're pretty far inside Tier territory now. I don't think we'll run into any Hyos unless they're swarming, in which case they won't stop to investigate a distress call."

"No shit," Falstaff conceded.

"Besides, there might be a *Katular* fighter about."

"Not according to the briefing you so carefully pointed out to me. They should all be picked up by now."

"Well, someone might have chosen to go home by a different route. Besides, even though you can't spare an erg, I've still got the energy to burn, so why not signal?"

"True. But we're so far off the shipping lanes, *Katular*'s got to be the only thing around to hear us, and it's much too far away."

"Maybe."

"You should go on ahead and try to reach it by yourself."

"If you saw my board, you wouldn't say that." There was more red and more FAIL indicators than Indiw had ever seen before. "This craft isn't going anywhere."

"You took more damage than you reported?"

"I don't know. I don't think so. But failures have been progressive. I still think we have a chance, though. Just go to sleep to conserve oxygen. They'll find us."

They exchanged a few more comments, then set their brain wave stimulators to induce deep coma. Indiw's last thought was of the land on Sinaha that might yet be his.

Only when, after a long, lazy return to consciousness, he opened his eyes on normal light did Indiw realize he hadn't seriously expected to live.

He was in the hospital aboard an Ardr ship.

The sounds were normal, the air pressure was normal, the symphony of smells was wholly reassuring, and the breeze was cool, unlike the still, stuffy heat of the human ship. A thousand cues he'd never been aware of before told his body he was safe.

The tree branches arching over his bed rustled—albeit in the artificial breeze—and rained aromatic pollen onto his skin that had been tortured by that awful uniform. It was bliss. A tiny fountain beside his bed trickled effervescent water. His bed was made of the finest white sand cupped in a pink granite bowl—so it was *fake* granite, it was still pure heaven after waking in that human hospital, coughing and vomiting from sheer subliminal terror, sicker from that than from ramming his fighter into the crash fields on *Tacoma*'s flight deck.

The healing tree had done its work well. He stretched, took a deep breath, and sat up, scrubbing the sand over his skin to cleanse away the last of the odor of illness. He could buff the scratches off later. Right now he wanted to feel clean. Then he plunged his head, horns first, into the depths of the fountain. He drank deeply, letting the bubbles stimulate his horns and cool the stiff crest between them until it resumed its brilliant whiteness. He even sucked some of the frothy stuff deep into his lungs. *Ah, wonderful!*

"Falstaff!" he whispered as he suddenly realized what this luxury must seem like to the human. And then he knew he really had expected to die out in space. When he'd proposed his scheme, he'd never given one thought to the consequences of success.

The human had tried to welcome Indiw to *Tacoma*. He had to make a similar effort for him, now. After all, it was his decision that had brought them both here. And he had to protect *Katular* from Falstaff—if he could.

He glanced at the hedges isolating him from the other patients in this public area. When he concentrated, he could make out the human scent, and that together with a trace of sound gave him the direction. The human issue uniform and flight suit he had worn had been taken away, but they'd left pilot's straps for him. He donned them hastily, buffed his hide to an even ruddy glow to be sure he was decent, fluffed his crest dry, then sidled through the hedge into the trail between treatment areas.

"How do you feel now?" a soft voice asked in the common language of the First Tier.

"Lousy. Don't you have something—anything—for a headache? Where are my clothes? And where's Indiw? You did pick him up, too, didn't you?"

Someone sighed, eloquently conveying relief and bafflement together.

Homing on the sound, Indiw plunged through the hedgerow and spoke before Falstaff could even see him. "Commander, I am here, and well, and pleased you have survived, too."

The staff people surrounding the bed at a proper reassuring distance turned on Indiw, crouched in defensive posture. Indiw apologized with a hasty gesture. They straightened, embarrassed at overreacting. Indiw slipped between them into Falstaff's personal space, knowing the staff's polite distance had only increased his tension and thus his pain.

They had stretched a piece of white material over the sand to try to give the human something familiar to lie on, and they'd turned off the wind so it was hot and stuffy. The healing tree's pollen was making a sticky mess out of the material.

The human's bare skin was covered with a sparse coat of short hair matted now by the pollen. His head hair was even worse. Falstaff was curled on one side, one knee raised, back twisted to expose only his bare flank and ribs to the pollen fall. It must feel like hell. He wondered if the strip of skin that was a lighter color was more sensitive. Though the pollen would do a human no biochemical harm, it surely wouldn't do any good either.

The tactile memory of the warm water shower the humans had made Indiw use in their hospital flattened his crest and told him instantly what to do for this man. "Sarlkin," he addressed the nearest specialist by title, "I am Indiw. This one needs warm water falling from above his height to cleanse himself, and his clothing must be cleaned and presented to him immediately. Then he must have food suitable for humans after a long fast, preferably warm food with hot drink. With this treatment and some conversation, his pain should subside."

"We are endeavoring to provide conversation, but I had forgotten about the water requirements of humans. Food is on the way to his quarters, and I will see that his clothing is readied. Tijutin, find a way to provide for his watering needs." The Sarlkin gestured his thanks to Indiw with a whole body move, and left, followed by the other technicians.

"Boy, am I glad to see you!" The human sank back in what appeared to be relief. One hand tried, in an apparently habitual but frustrated gesture, to flip the cloth around himself. It was, however, anchored firmly. He rested his head on the crook of one elbow and commented, "I wouldn't have recognized you out of uniform. Do you remember anything that happened?" He felt his head again, and muttered, "I'm not used to waking up in a ship's hospital, hurting."

"I remember nothing after we engaged the brain wave regulators until I woke up here a few minutes ago. If the pain is great, perhaps there is more wrong than simple oxygen deprivation?"

"Not that bad, really. How long were we out? There isn't even a clock in here."

With his back to the fountain, the human was looking right at the instrument panel and didn't even recognize it. Indiw stepped closer into the human's space, wondering why he was still just lying there. Perhaps he was more ill than he sounded? He knelt to open the instrument panel and expose the bedside services monitor and the clock. "About, hmmm, twelve hours since we started to coast toward *Katular*. So we must have been here, oh, maybe four hours."

"So by now somebody must have told *Tacoma* we're here. Who would be in charge of that? How can we verify that the message was sent?"

A few days ago Indiw would never have been able to understand the helplessness the human had to be feeling. But his own experiences had given him a new perspective. Indiw punched up the Communications Roster to see who had volunteered to handle traffic today. He got the name of the responsible party, entered the query, and got a negative even before Falstaff became impatient for an answer.

"No message about us has been sent to *Tacoma*. Would you like to word that message yourself?"

"Nobody told them we'd been picked up? How could that be?"

"I don't know. Is it important? I could find out."

"Don't bother. Just have somebody tell *Tacoma* we're all right—can we get a status report on our fighters to send with the message? Are they repairable? How long until we can get out of here?"

Indiw concluded the human was actually in better shape than he himself was, for Indiw's own brain was not yet functioning on that level. He was still in shock from finding himself alive—and with the responsibility for a very lost human trying to survive in an Ardr environment.

But even as Falstaff spoke, he was entering the queries and getting what answers *Katular* had on file. "Minimum repair time on yours, six days. Mine may be ready before that. Since we were hospitalized, our fighters weren't put on priority. I'll append that to the message to *Tacoma*."

He reduced the information to the telegraphic syntax used by the Tier fleets and put it in the com hopper. "The message will go out in, oh, approximately three hours."

"Ha. Meanwhile, we're AWOL. I wonder how Chancy's taking it?"

The drop in the human's tone of voice alerted Indiw to the possibility of a slide into depression. "I will apply for a priority status on our repairs since we're uninjured," he said, doing it, "and then I'll go and see about expediting that shower for you—and your clothing."

While he was about it, he called up the space allocation listing and found that the medical department had subject-to-approval holds on two places for them on the pilot's deck. "Look, they've gotten us quarters next to each other. Here's a visual of your place. See if it suits you. You can always choose any other vacant place, but all the ones on the pilot's deck are apt to be similar. Order any special equipment you'd like while I go get things moving."

"Hey, you're a patient here, too. You can't just wander out."

"Why not? I'm fine." He was all the way out in the public corridor before he recalled how upset the human medics had been when he'd gone looking for work. Left to himself, the human would remain in the hospital until people thought him not quite sane. There were a lot of things not in the cross-species manuals!

He found the Sarlkin supervising the setup of a freestanding shower stall in the quarters they'd claimed for the human. A small heating unit was being spliced into the water lines to provide warmed water. The techs argued about what temperature to set it for, with the Sarlkin insisting it shouldn't be more than the temperature of human blood.

Indiw described the shower in the human hospital, and the engineer went in search of a water mixing valve and some more pipe. Falstaff's flight suit, cleaned but looking rather odd, was folded over a seating unit beside his fountain. It was damp from the spray. He moved it close to an air vent to dry. A large cloth had been provided to cover the sand bed. When he checked, Indiw found that Falstaff had rapidly conquered the ship's system and ordered several more cloths and some soft padding.

Exploring his own quarters, Indiw found a basic issue wardrobe and grooming kit. He snatched up the large, shapeless drape ordinarily worn to contain one's scent during sexual arousal and went back to the hospital.

Very carefully not mentioning what the garment was usually for, he said, "Here, put this on. By the time we get to your quarters, the shower should be ready, and by then your clothing will be dry."

That trip with Falstaff through ordinary ship's corridors was the most memorable of his life. He recalled the wide, brightly lit, often jam-packed halls of *Tacoma* and saw the narrow, dark, deserted spaces through human eyes. *Tacoma* and *Katular* were identical in hull manufacture, but the humans carved their interiors into tiny sleeping compartments and huge, open gathering spots. Ardr put most of their space into individual living units, and very little into public space—except necessary working areas and the mating area that on a carrier like this would be lavish. *Don't even think about that! Not now.*

He got his charge installed in quarters duly equipped and supplied with several shipping crates of emergency rations rated for humans. Of course, *Tacoma* had not offered him anything better. But the medics had managed to provide heating equipment for the food.

The engineers, medics, and service crew were all clearing out of the human's place as Indiw and Falstaff arrived. With apologetic gestures for having intruded, which Indiw accepted gracefully on Falstaff's behalf, the crew hurried away.

"Well, come on in, close the door," said Falstaff as he advanced on the pile of clothing. "Lord, what a mess." He picked up his uniform and shook it. "These uniforms don't need pressing! Well, I'll manage." Then he turned and saw Indiw still politely beyond the threshold. "Don't just stand there. It's drafty. Come in."

"Uh, one doesn't intrude into the private space of another.

And, hmmm, I—uh—" His eyes flicked in the direction of his own place.

"Ah, it's been a while since you've been alone," said Falstaff with a nod. "Sorry, you've been through worse than I have the last couple of days. Go on. I'll get this all figured out. Just—ah—where do you suppose they've put the services monitor in here?"

"Right by your left hand. There's a plant tendril that needs trimming growing down over it."

"In here?" He fumbled the panel open. "Fine. I'm set. Go get some rest. If nothing else, I can do some gardening!"

Indiw hoped that was a joke signaling the lifting of the impending depression. "I'll call you to be sure you know how to call me. Just a minute."

He went into his own quarters and closed the door, putting his privacy lock code into it. Then he went to his own panel, dropped into the seat with an astonishing sense of relief washing through his knees, and entered Falstaff's room designation. "Pilot Commander Falstaff?"

"Walt," the human corrected, his viewer shimmering on and finally focusing. "After all this, surely you can call me Walt?"

"If that would please you, Walt." Indiw gave him the code designation for his own quarters, then waited while the human ran the connection for himself. "Good. Now I will get some rest. But don't—whatever you do—*don't* go wandering off through the ship by yourself. When you're ready to go out, call me." He could imagine what would happen if Falstaff drifted into some private worship service or worse yet the mating area.

Indiw tamed his imagination and devoted himself to an evening of creature comforts, of food that nourished spirit as well as body, of space that didn't echo with the scents of others, space he could make his own. It was emotionally overwhelming, and the sheer magnitude of the physical reaction and the severe fatigue that followed told him how close to the edge he had come. *What must Falstaff be going through?*

Indiw woke groggily to the com signal, dunked his head in his bedside fountain, shook, and rolled to his feet. It was twelve hours since he'd fallen asleep. He knew who it had to be on the com. And sure enough, it was Falstaff.

"Good morning, Walt," he said in the exact tone he'd learned from a language drill.

"How can you tell it's morning? The clock goes around three times for every day."

That's not why he's calling. "See where the little red dot is displayed? First position is morning, the second afternoon, the third night. But I know it's morning because I just woke up."

The human laughed. *That's a good sign.*

"Sorry I woke you, but listen, Indiw, I've been playing with this monitor for hours. Every time I think I've got it whipped, I discover I was all wrong. So I need some help. Can you come over here?"

"I'd rather not," he said without thinking, then regretted it. The human needed his space invaded, though Indiw needed his solitude. "But if you really want me to—"

"Oh, well, I wouldn't want to—"

Indiw felt ashamed. It was bad enough forcing the human to ask for help, then on top of that, he refused to give it. "I'm starved, and I need some time to wake up. Give me an hour or so, and I'll come see what your problem is."

"Fair enough. See you then. Now, how do you shut this down?" He fumbled and the screen went blank.

Actually, that was encouraging. If Falstaff had been playing with the services access, he hadn't gone wandering. Maybe they could get him back to *Tacoma* without a major interstellar incident.

It took Indiw twice as long as he'd estimated to get ready to take on the challenges his imagination served up based on his own adventures, but finally he presented himself at Falstaff's door. Glancing up and down the corridor to make sure nobody was around to observe, he slipped in as soon as the human opened it.

He showed him how to personalize his lock code, then Falstaff led him to the monitor. "Look what I found. It's some kind of note about your shipmates on *Tacoma*, but I couldn't make out what it—"

"Huuuu!"

"What?"

Indiw reached across and tapped in a code, holding his breath. Then he swore blisteringly as he stifled a raw emotional surge. He lunged to his feet and retreated as far from the human as he could, struggling to master his shock.

CHAPTER
THREE

★

WHILE INDIW STRUGGLED FALSTAFF WAITED, PATIENTLY
at first and then with growing concern. Indiw pulled himself
together and explained, "They're dead. I'm the only survivor
of *Katukin*."

The human made an inarticulate sound and whipped around
to stare at the display. He could read some Ardr words when
spelled out, but symbols and abbreviations no doubt were a
mystery to him. He hadn't realized the posting had been a
death notice.

Indiw forced his paralyzing shock aside, and walked back
to sit by the human, pointing out the revealing symbols. "The
others died in the hospital aboard *Tacoma*. Your Captain has
signaled that *Katular* should send a party to pick up the
bodies."

"Shit. They were friends of yours? I'm sorry, Indiw."

Indiw summoned patience. "I knew them, yes. But—"

"Look, we'll light a fire under the engineers to get our fighters ready. Somehow we'll wangle our way into the pickup
party. They deserve to have a friend among their pallbearers.
That way, I can get back to *Tacoma*, and you can return with
your own people. Now, who do we talk to in order to get
ourselves assigned to this mission?"

As he spoke, Falstaff had pulled up the roster, but obviously didn't know what to do with it. Indiw took the controls,

pretending his fingers weren't shaking. He'd never be able to explain that his reaction wasn't grief but shock at finding himself the *only* survivor, and what that portended for his future if and when anyone noticed.

Being a lone survivor could make his career provided it didn't seem he'd been deranged by it.

He told the human, "You don't 'get assigned.' And you don't need anyone's permission. Attitudes like that will make everyone uncomfortable with you."

Falstaff nodded as if suddenly understanding.

Indiw called up the progress records on the repairs to their fighters. He looked over what the engineers had done, and what remained to be done, then he found the priority assignment list and saw what jobs the engineers had on their lists ahead of their craft.

Using the ship's repair estimating program, he figured how soon their fighters could be ready if they were on the list for the mission to *Tacoma*. With the upped priority, they could gain maybe a day. "So. If the mission flies two days from now, we can be on it. And it makes sense that you should go with this group, to return you to your base ship. See, there are still swarms active in the area—will be for weeks yet. Nobody should fly alone."

Even as he spoke, the ship vibrated with the rhythmic thump-whoosh of fighters launching. A crawl across the bottom of the monitor silently announced their mission.

"Can we use that as an argument?"

Against whom? Indiw despaired of explaining. "Watch." He called up the missions listing, found that the one to *Tacoma* hadn't even been entered yet, and made the entry using the departure time when they could be ready, then cross-referenced it to Engineering so they'd get their priority raised. He put their names on top of the list, then flagged the listing so *Tacoma* would be notified when the appropriate number of pilots had volunteered. Fighters couldn't bring back cargo so someone had to volunteer to nurse a cargo transport through the combat zone.

"If too many people want to go, we may get bumped off by those with more weight. Those with outstanding records in their jobs get first choice on anything they want to do. I have no standing on this ship; neither do you. And someone with more weight might want to go sooner than we can."

Indiw showed the human how to call up the mission listing to check on it. "If the mission list locks in with you still on it, your monitor will automatically show it flashing on the screen even if the screen is off. Then you have to respond like this. See?"

Falstaff sat nodding silently at the monitor, lips pressed hard together. After a while, Indiw asked, "What are you thinking?"

"That Captain Sutcliff must be sitting on *Tacoma*'s bridge, gnashing his teeth in frustration at having to deal with an Ardr ship that won't even answer a summons to pick up crew. I'll bet *Tacoma* asked for someone to come get them while they were still alive."

"Possibly. But they were *Katukin* crew so probably no one on *Katular* was responsible."

"Do you suppose the message just sat here in the computer and nobody even put it on the missions listing?"

"Could be."

"God, Indiw! How can you be so cold! They were your own wing's last survivors! They might have lived if anyone here had gotten off their butt to come get them!"

It was a thought that had preyed on Indiw's mind every moment since they'd been picked up by the humans. The first thing he'd done when he woke on *Tacoma* was to send his own messages to *Katular* to ask for a medevac for his fellows, but no one on *Katular* was obligated to him personally, and being unlanded, he had no neighbors, thus no power.

What could he possibly say? Could he put the human's mind at rest by pointing out that his fellows, like himself, were not yet landed and so their deaths didn't count for much? He knew enough about humans to know that the explanation would just revolt Falstaff. "I know, Walt. It could easily have been me lying there in *Tacoma*'s sickbay subjected to—all that meticulous care. Dying."

"Oh, shit. I didn't mean—look, forget I mentioned it. Humans and Ardr are always going to be frustrated with each other's ways of doing things. And Lord knows, I can't complain at how you've all treated me."

"Speaking of treating you," Indiw said, pushing his seat back from the monitor display, "it's time to take you on a tour of the ship, show you where not to go so you can wander around by yourself. I had nightmares last night figuring you'd go exploring out of restlessness."

"Nightmares?"

"Don't ask." He led the way to the door, saying, "Check the corridor. I don't want anyone to see me coming out of your place. I've got enough trouble already."

"Trouble?"

I've got to learn to watch my mouth! He grabbed a ship's map from the rack by the door, and ducked out when Falstaff gave the all clear. He lit the map screen and began marking in the common Tier symbols. "Here we are, see? Now I want you to mark each of the places I point out to you." He handed the human the device, and led off. "You do understand why I couldn't do this for you in your room?"

"Sort of. I remember that Ardr use scent markings instead of printed signs. So you have to go find the signs to tell me about them. But they change all the time, so—"

"Well, I'm just going to warn you off *all* the tricky spots, even the public toilets, leaving nothing to your judgment. If you're smart enough to follow my advice, it'll keep you out of trouble." He noticed the human's expression shift. "Is something wrong?"

"I'm lecturing myself on how Ardr aren't really arrogant and uncaring, but just tend to hit the wrong cues in humans—like when I clapped you on the shoulder to say I was glad to have you flying with me, and you about ripped my guts out."

Indiw searched for a proper expression of chagrin and found one of Falstaff's favorites. "Shit! I'm sorry, I don't even know what I said wrong. I just know that you'd hate to stay inside for two or three more days."

"And you'd like to do just that."

"With one or two possible exceptions, yes." Before the human could ask about *that,* Indiw pointed out a room that was used as a place of worship by several of the religions aboard *Katular.* "And before you ask, no, I don't know anything about their practices or beliefs. My tradition is very different. *That* corridor goes to the hospital, if you need anything from the medics. They can expedite all kinds of things for you. Mark it."

Indiw tried to keep the human busy and focused on learning the ship rather than on asking for a complete explication of Ardr customs. An hour later they arrived at the main bridge. The female running the ship today—whom those on *Tacoma* would have called Captain—welcomed the pilots on tour, but since she was new to the job, it took her several minutes to adjust the Winslow Security screens to pass a human through.

While she was struggling with it, Falstaff said, "Look, I've seen enough bridges. I was a carrier pilot once. We don't have to—"

Indiw whispered, "It would be rude not to visit the bridge. It's a public area. Neither one of us has ever been on this ship before."

"Oh. Well. In that case. Sure."

Triumphant over the security system, the Captain of *Katular* graciously showed them around, making certain that Falstaff touched each of the consoles. She discoursed at length on the intricacies of the ten stations that combined to command the carrier, then said, pointing out the informational displays, "We're still heading toward *Tacoma,* which is headed away from us. We're expecting heavy action soon, so all our reconnaissance equipment is deployed."

They discussed the tactical situation until management details distracted her. Exiting the bridge on the other side of the ship, they headed back toward the pilot's deck. "Gymnastic equipment is through that door. You're welcome to use what you can of it, but ask before you touch anything. Some things might have reserve flashings you wouldn't notice until you had someone angry at you—who'd then be very embarrassed at having been angry."

"Do you suppose there's a pool?"

"Pool of what?"

"Water. A swimming pool? Good aerobic exercise."

"Oh. *No.*" There weren't even any human women on this ship and he was asking such a question! "Come on, there's something else I have to show you here." He pushed the gym door open.

It was a typical ship's gym, with areas marked off by lush greenery. "Only one person at a time in each of the marked areas. Except to be sure that you aren't taking someone's reserved place—don't talk in here at all."

They crossed through on the central path to the door on the other side, the inconspicuous, carefully unmarked door. He explained it was an automated door that would open when someone stepped up to it, so it would never be touched, never gain anyone's scent markings. "And you must not either touch it or trigger it open."

Falstaff made a mark on his map as Indiw steered him away from the door so it wouldn't appear they were discussing it—and they wouldn't be blocking the way for anyone who needed access.

"Indiw, the map says there's a big area between this door and the other longitudinal corridor we used to go forward—almost the entire central core of the ship is a single, long open space, and it's not marked Engineering."

"Will your curiosity make you investigate despite my warning?" He kept his voice low, hoping nobody would hear.

Falstaff considered that for an extended moment. "You don't want to discuss it. All right, maybe some other time. Meanwhile, I'll stay clear."

"Good, because if you don't, you could get yourself disemboweled." He flexed his claws in emphasis. Not to mention causing endless interstellar legal complications for the disemboweler and possibly all *Katular. No, not even a human could be that stupid.* Then Indiw remembered Chancy. "Walt, can I really trust you on this? It's very important."

Casting one last thoughtful glance at the inconspicuous door, Falstaff nodded. "My word on it. Good enough?"

"Good enough."

They continued their tour in Engineering where they watched the repairs on the fighters and talked with those managing the work today.

Indiw found his own fighter up on supports, belly plate panels removed, and almost all the weapons control circuitry gone. An engineer came over to him carrying a charred circuit board. "I'd sure like to know what did this. I didn't think it was possible to back overloads through here."

Indiw wasn't about to advertise his problematic conduct while bringing Falstaff in. He agreed, "It *was* a terrific battle."

The engineer said mournfully, "It's going to take me all day just to assemble the replacement parts."

Indiw commiserated, then said, "I wonder if you could remove that paint the humans used."

"I was planning to. It *is* ghastly, especially streaked and blistered like that. You'll be gleaming when you leave."

"That's a relief." They traded names and Indiw promised to register an approval for the engineer's work. It would put him just a little closer to becoming landed, but maybe the engineer would become a neighbor, not a rival. He had to start thinking about finding new neighbors who'd accept him. Everyone he knew was dead. He knew he should be thinking about reorganizing his affairs, but he just couldn't.

Falstaff approached as he spoke to the engineer. The human looked over the scarring on Indiw's fighter. The engineer asked Indiw affably, "Should I put *Katular*'s insignia on for you?"

"I'll let you know when I decide."

With Falstaff, he walked back to the human's craft, which had been entirely disassembled and strewn over a work surface. The human asked with intense curiosity, "I keep forgetting you won't simply be assigned a new post. How do you make up your mind? How do you arrange to join a wing?"

"By reviewing their battles, checking to see if they think the same way I do. I might take a current briefing dump, figure what I would do if I were flying the mission, and then watch to see how they deploy themselves—then review the records afterward to see what they did. If I decide I fit in, then I have to convince them to give me a chance. They might let me fly a training sortie with them, and if I weave pattern with them comfortably—I'll go into combat with them."

"You mean you guys don't just fly around in random circles until you've killed all the enemy?"

"Is that what it looks like to you?" *Amazing.* "No, it isn't random. But to know what to do and when to do it, you have to think exactly the same as everyone else in your wing, getting the same answers to every problem you work. A really perfect match is very, very rare—" He broke off, suddenly overcome with loss.

Quietly Falstaff said, "And that's what you had on *Katukin.*" He chewed on his lower lip. "I'm sorry for reminding you again." With a cryptic gesture, he turned to one of the engineers working on the pieces of his fighter and launched into a technical discussion. Indiw could well imagine the sudden sense of urgency the human felt to get home where people reacted normally and things could be accomplished without thinking much about them.

He left Falstaff in Engineering, happily discovering that here engineers delighted in having the pilots oversee the work on their own fighters.

Indiw made his way back to his own place thinking about that anonymous door on the inner wall of the gym and the receptive females who would be prowling beyond it. Could he possibly slip away while Falstaff was busy? But he should be digging into the records to find himself a new position. And he had to check on the *Tacoma* mission listing. He thought about all the things he should be doing, and decided to go walking first. With Falstaff on his hands, he might not get another chance.

But no, it was not to be. His monitor was blinking when he came in. Now that everyone doing Mission Review had seen his flight recordings, three Reviewers had called for a public Interview. Three! He'd known he'd be in trouble. He hadn't thought it would be this bad, though.

He'd done nothing to attract such attention. He should have been absorbed onto *Katular* routinely, coming to notice only when they found out how good a pilot he was. Something really unusual was up. It wasn't just his being the lone survivor of *Katukin.* That would have warranted one Interviewer, maybe two, not three. Three was trouble. Three was *T*rouble.

He groomed more meticulously than he had since he'd first presented himself for Pilot's Training. He polished his hide to a ruddy glow, not showing a scratch. He whitened his crest, and honed his hand and toe claws. He scrubbed off every bit of stray scent and used inhibitors to be sure he didn't offend anyone—especially females. He even dosed the scent glands between his toes so he could wear sandals, exposing his claws as befitted someone ready to be landed.

He polished his pilot's straps and inspected his appearance. His fatigue and tension still showed around the eyes, but he couldn't do anything about that now. This Interview would go on record for anyone to call up—for the rest of his life and maybe beyond. He'd done his best; it would just have to be good enough.

Courage in hand, he took himself to the Interview room, one of those places he'd put on Falstaff's restricted list.

The three Interviewers waited for him, poised and ready to begin. At least his timing was impeccable. The female was the most junior among them, young—beautiful. It was a good thing he'd poured on the scent inhibitor. The other two were males older than Indiw, polished and perfectly groomed.

Silently promising himself they wouldn't see him so much as twitch under the female's gaze, Indiw took his seat. The two people running the recorders laid identifying plaques before the Interviewers, then settled at their monitoring stations. The female Interviewer was Shusdim, an exercise trainer. The older male was Amscill, a xenologist. And the other male was Fikkhor, a medic. Both males were landed.

Shusdim faced the recorder in front of her and recited the names and accreditations of the three Interviewers. Since this was also available live to any monitor on the ship, she asked the distant audience if anyone would care to replace one of them.

There were a few bids, but after some discussion the job still fell to the three in the room. Indiw concentrated as he usually did only in battle, knowing that his whole future revolved around this. Still, when the first question came, he was at a loss.

"Why did you elect to fly with the humans?" asked one of the males—the older one whose crest had begun to darken.

But that's perfectly obvious.

"Do you choose not to answer?" asked the female.

"I will answer." He told them of waking in the *Tacoma* sickbay, of his frustration as everything he did rammed him into one obtuse human custom or another, and how he'd won through to the information that *Tacoma* was about to mount the ground strike that had been *Katukin's* responsibility.

"I could not let the humans alone defend the planet on which I hope to settle."

"But you knew you would have to take oath to fly with them according to their customs. What made you think that you *could* keep that oath, once taken?" Amscill's shrewd, dark suspicion was reflected in the others' eyes.

Outraged, Indiw glared at Amscill. "I have never broken an oath!" Their eyes locked in combat for one powerful moment.

Most of Indiw's career records, except the most recent, had survived *Katukin* because they'd been routinely filed at planetary bases, but the Interviewers had no way to verify his words now. With no other survivor available to vouch for him, he had to convince them of his character on his bare word. Later, when his records arrived, it might go a little better with him, but this impression of him would dominate.

Indiw transferred his gaze to his hands, carefully, formally flexed his claws and retracted them. "I chose to keep that oath. It was the price I had to pay to defend what will one day be my land. Is there any price too great for that?" His voice shook with passion, and he let it show for they would think he meant the terrible price of conforming to human custom, fighting pack style, but in fact the greater price had been the loss of his wing.

He raised his eyes. The unlanded female nodded first, but the males also remembered all too well how it had been for them, and soon agreed. Land was priceless.

They went on to examine Indiw's flight recordings, those made during his last mission out of *Katukin,* those of the battle for *Katukin* in progress when he returned, and lastly those made during his flight with Pit Bull Squadron. Each image, each exchange with the human pilots, and each maneuver were minutely questioned.

And their specific fear became evident. Any Ardr who was capable of allying with humans, partaking of the pack mentality in battle no less, could be the first traitor, the one who revealed to the humans how to subjugate Ardr. No one doubted that whether the humans themselves knew it or not, subjugation or eradication of all Ardr was indeed the humans' goal.

Every Ardr who studied humans even in passing knew that eventually it would come to an all-out human/Ardr war, perhaps a genocidal war of extinction in which no one could predict what the Fornak would do.

No one wanted such a war, but no one had yet come up with any way of avoiding it. Only facing the Hyos as a common enemy had postponed it this long.

They probed Indiw's reasons for staying with Falstaff's crippled vessel. They dug at his motives for originating and implementing an utterly foolhardy method of propelling the disabled human craft toward *Katular.* He inferred that Shusdim had certainly been a combat pilot herself. And she was the most suspicious.

They had nothing but the usual unalloyed praise for his performance both in the attack on the swarm and his later defense of *Katukin*. It was easy to turn their questions back on them. He had fit into his wing so well, combat had become a sweetness most people never experienced and could never comprehend. His loss was irreplaceable, and very few, not even Shusdim, could even perceive that it was a loss. He knew it would be a very private ache that would live in him for the rest of his life.

When the Interviewers got into his flight with Pit Bull, he had to explain decisions that had come from he-knew-not-where inside himself. Often he had to say, "I chose," in a tone that truncated the discussion with a privacy barrier.

They made him relive the entire experience. And it was far more disturbing in retrospect than it had been to race through it, putting each moment behind as it passed and mentally grabbing at the next moment, hoping only to survive.

When no one could think of any more questions, the elder male, Amscill, asked, as if musing aloud, "Indiw, have you ever heard the human term, *hero*?"

"Yes, though I can't claim to understand it."

"They believe it is a good thing to be," said Fikkhor.

"But they also say it is better to be a live coward than a dead hero, and coward isn't a good thing to be," said Indiw. "So maybe hero isn't, either." He remembered Chancy's parting admonition to Falstaff, *"Don't be a hero."*

Shusdim added with feminine distaste, "Both terms are derived from their pack mentality. What Ardr could ever understand *that*?"

Amscill observed, "The hero manifestation of the pack mentality makes humans the most formidable threat Ardr have ever faced. It's not nearly so common among the Fornak."

Indiw commented, "I don't think we can ever understand humans. They're not at all like the pack hunters we conquered on our own world who had no concept of territory. Humans understand territory and the defense of it. One gains access to a human's territory only by invitation, while at the same time they enjoy 'entertaining'—that is, inviting others into their territory—and 'visiting'—invading another's territory." He gestured bewilderment. "It twists your brains to try to imagine human motives. They're unpredictable, savage, unprincipled, and devoid of all sense of decency." *But they make hellishly good pilots!*

"That's another reason they're potentially the most dangerous threat Ardr have ever faced," said Shusdim. "If we understood them, we might have a chance against them."

Fikkhor mused, "I have observed three kinds of hero: the one who deliberately does something suicidal that buys life for others, the one who risks his life and pays dearly but survives to see what his suffering has bought for others, and the one who does something utterly stupid yet survives unscathed to watch others benefit from his action. No hero was ever proclaimed for acting to gain land for his own personal, exclusive, and private use.

"This Interview was deemed necessary because *Tacoma*'s Captain has informed us that you are to be awarded one of their decorations for heroism. Though it is their way of expressing approval, you can well understand why any sane person might be hesitant about serving with you after this— escapade—coming right on the heels of your being the sole survivor of *Katukin*.

"Anyone might suspect that your survival, *unwounded,* of two winning battles in which your side was nearly wiped out had wakened in you—goralchor."

The medic delivered the last word in the hushed tone of one diagnosing a fatal disease. And indeed it could be, for goralchor was the survivor's complex, the sense of absolute invincibility that inevitably led to disaster.

Indiw remembered Falstaff's flippant *"Don't you know I'm invincible?"* Suppose Falstaff was overheard saying that here?

He dared not let his claws flex, but his whole body was throbbing with fear-fight-flight responses, all mixed and colliding with each other. He'd never in his worst nightmares believed he could be in this much trouble. He schooled his voice, and tried to sound sane as he asked, "Would it be possible to refuse the . . . honor the humans are offering?"

"Is that what you choose to do?"

Would it cause political problems between Ardr and humans? No, it had to be just a minor honor in a minor battle awarded to a person of no consequence. Who would even notice? "Yes. I am here to defend the land I *can only hope* one day to occupy myself." He emphasized the words to indicate he felt no invincible certainty of surviving to become landed. "May I point out that when I chose to fly with the humans, I knew only that my fellow pilots were wounded. I did not expect to become the sole survivor."

Indiw sat outwardly composed as they called for questions from the listeners—and there were a few, most notably from the engineer who'd been working on Indiw's craft and who wanted a reprise of the sequence where Indiw had nudged Falstaff's fighter into a vector change.

When they'd gone through it in minute detail, the engineer concluded, "It was the proximity of the other shields that caused the backflow into the control circuits. I couldn't have predicted that. I don't think a pilot would have, not while intent on accomplishing the maneuver. The only way he could have made it work was to get that close and use such low power that the weapons systems would take that kind of backflow. I want this maneuver listed as suicidal so no one else will make the same mistake Indiw did."

Mistake! Relief swept through Indiw at the exoneration.

After a short discussion, the engineer won his point.

It didn't affect the heroism accusation, since he'd stood accused of stupidity not suicide or greed. But they proceeded on the assumption that if he had known what the maneuver would do to his craft, he wouldn't have tried to save Falstaff. Indiw was not so sure.

He kept thinking about Falstaff popping the Hyos that was after him, the one he'd never even seen. It was very clear on the recordings they'd just watched, though no one remarked on it. Maybe they didn't know the human formation patterns well enough to discern the risk Falstaff had taken to protect his—alien—wingman.

The three times they'd played it back, Indiw had watched the sequence transfixed by a growing certainty that Falstaff had *known* that Indiw, irrevocably committed to his dive-and-climb maneuver, had been unaware of the threat on his tail. Falstaff moved his fighter around Indiw's with deft confidence, as if he'd written the program for the maneuver.

Later, there had been the times Indiw had taken out Hyos who attacked Falstaff. In the growing heat of battle, Indiw had forgotten everything he'd memorized about fighting formations. Yet he had *known* what Falstaff was about to do.

Eventually, the Interviewers decided they had everything on record, and Indiw was free to go. With an effort, he pulled out of the shivering realization that a human could fly like an Ardr while thinking Ardr flew at random. Then he presented his leave-taking with all proper formalities, communicating an appropriate sense of vulnerability with every subtle trick of body language he knew. But if they understood how vulnerable he really felt, they might disqualify him as a pilot.

He went back to his place to do some research and plan how to salvage the rest of his life.

So far, the *Tacoma* mission had attracted three volunteers, but even as Indiw watched the screen, the names were withdrawn. However, he had noted them. He looked them up. They were all pilots who flew with *Katular*'s First Wing.

He began his research with the Second Wing, which was in

space right now. Almost immediately, he knew he could never fly with them—too much temperament. So he tried the Third. They were mostly female pilots, and a goodly number of them senior enough to be near retirement. There would be opportunity for advancement with the Third Wing. For a few years, he might accommodate himself to their conservative tactics. The first wing he'd chosen had flown like that. He knew he could do it, and he could even excel.

The Fourth Wing was composed exclusively of two related religious groups, neither of which attracted Indiw. They would not be interested in him.

He focused his efforts on the Third, assessing their prior battles, studying their style. If they'd consider him despite the stigma the humans had laid on him, he might just have found a new home.

But even at that discovery, his spirits didn't recover.

He looked in a mirror and the tension lines around his eyes told him what he needed, a little therapeutic exercise followed by a walk. He certainly couldn't present himself to the Third Wing in such volatile condition.

He took a good sand-scrubbing, oiled away the scent inhibitor from all strategic locations, donned his loose walking robe, and opened his door.

As he stepped out, Falstaff was coming out of his own door. The human hailed him with a nerve-shattering whistle. "Wait up!" The human closed the distance between them pushing his light-altering goggles into place. "Where you going all dressed up?"

"For a walk. I'll see you when I get back." The human reeked of mixed human odors.

"Did anyone sign up to go to *Tacoma* yet?"

"There was no one else on the list a few moments ago."

"Mind if I tag along?"

"Yes." He turned away and moved off at a good stride

flexing his claws to relieve tension.

The human took one step after him, and checked, hand out, a bewildered "Hey—" dying on his lips.

Indiw, realizing the human hadn't understood, went back. "I'm not angry with you. I just need a couple of hours. I'll come to your place and we'll work on getting some pilots to go to *Tacoma*."

"I'm sorry if I've been a burden. . . ."

"Not that." The image of that Hyos exploding behind him, unseen, was too vivid in memory. "Never that. I just need to take a walk."

"Okay. See you later." The human went back to his own door, and Indiw, relieved that he'd finally communicated, went on up the passageway to the cross-corridor that led to a side door of the gym.

He claimed an area, set up music for rhythm, focused the speakers so no one else would be bothered, kicked off his sandals, and put everything he had into a stretching and bending drill that segued into his combat moves. Spinning, kicking, rolling, gutting imaginary enemies with feet and hands, he finished with a good run on a high gravity treadmill to dispel the ache in his claws for warm entrails and blood.

When he felt in control, he dismounted, triggered the timer to cleanse the area of his scent, and made his way to the unmarked door. After the Interview this afternoon, he had little chance of succeeding on a walk, and he wasn't used to that anymore. Rejection could be agonizing, embarrassing, and he could end up more tense than he was now. He'd been an adult too long to have much tolerance for that state.

But if he was going to try to live on this ship, he had to prove to at least one female that he wasn't goralchor. And he didn't know any other way to do that.

As he paused letting the door open in front of him, he nervously scanned behind him. Over a nearby hedge, a pale oval rose into sight followed by a dark-clad body. A human body. Falstaff. The human stopped with his weight supported on straightened arms, his legs pointing to either side of his body. He must have swung up on a crossbar not meant to be climbed on, but there wasn't any harm in it. He just looked silly.

In the instant Indiw's eyes focused on him, Falstaff swung his torso up and back, legs following, and held himself upside down on his fully extended arms, the back of his head to Indiw, balanced only on his hands. It looked dangerous and sickening, but he seemed to be enjoying it. It was probably some sort of mating display. Fortunately, there were no humans around.

At least Falstaff hadn't dislocated his shoulders, for even as Indiw stepped through the open door, the human reversed position so his face was toward Indiw, braced the bottoms of his feet on the bar beside his hands and swung out of sight, rear end leading.

The door closed, cutting off Indiw's view before he was sure whether the human had seen him. But then the sensory riot of the inner walkway claimed him: the vocalizations of females announcing his arrival in guarded tones, the odor of fresh water, huge trees with sap-soaked bark, fragrant flowers, rich loam, the delightful sound of songbirds, an entire homeworld ecology—or at least the impression of one.

Forgetting Falstaff, Indiw stuffed his robe into the receptacle by the door. He felt his crest spreading, his spine straightening. He followed the males' path onto the main concourse and turned to walk the length of the mating area.

He had thought it would be lavish. It exceeded his expectations. The rooms dotted along both sides of the long walkway were large, well spaced, very private. He paused to look through one open door and eyed the deep pond, the perfect fine white sand, the dual private toilet facilities, and the decorations illustrating fascinating embellishments two young enthusiasts might try.

He strolled on, imagination fired by the scent of eager females in the concealing shrubbery. But none chose him. After the initial announcement of his coming, none so much as breathed as he passed.

Distantly he heard the entry door open and close, and tensed for the commotion that would erupt if Falstaff had followed him. But the silence proclaimed it to be another female— one who might be interested? He thought about his pride, and then about his need, and decided that if no one chose him by the time he reached the exit, he'd walk back, give them all another good look. After all, he was new and had a reputation to overcome and one to build.

Yes, one more pass. But just one. He dared not assert his own choice until he had been chosen by at least three different females and satisfied them fully. Otherwise, he might find himself in one of those rooms, disemboweled. If he lingered here too long unchosen, he knew his resolve would waver. One more pass. No more. He'd been an adult long enough to know his limits.

He came to the end where the exit was ringed by artificial stone providing many comfortable ledges. He claimed one and stretched out casually, as if his mind were more on exploring than mating. If he was only going to allow himself one more pass up the walk, he should wait awhile so there might be more new females to see him.

He lay in a worn niche just above floor level, and drank in the ambience of the place.

He had drowsed into a lovely fantasy when a warm body intruded into his space, a female body. He looked up, hardly daring to move as her scent swirled around him making his horns tingle and a rumble ignite deep in his chest.

She was lean, voluptuous, filling the senses. She was wanting ferociously, but gazed down at him with hard eyes. She hadn't chosen yet.

She studied him. He moved to expose himself fully to her view, bidding with all the subtle power of maleness.

She studied every inch of him, her body saying she was only looking while her scent told him she was frantic.

When he trembled on the brink of choosing her and losing all hope of gaining respect on this ship forever, she gestured briskly and turned to lead him into the nearest vacant room.

He surrendered to his glands. It was glorious. It was everything he needed it to be. They finished, splashing in the pond, exulting in the silky warmth of the water, wholly satisfied.

Resting on the bottom, with the water up around his neck, and the female straddling him, toying with his hypersensitized horns, he asked languorously, "Why? Why did you choose me? Hadn't you heard?"

"I saw the Interview. Considering how you fly, I did not think you would live long enough for me to have another chance—maybe for anyone to have another chance." She rose, levered herself out of the pond, and rolled into the sand to cleanse and dry. "I like unique experiences. And this one was—singular indeed. But—you didn't turn out to be quite what I expected. So maybe I will see you again."

If she thought she'd have a chance to choose him again, had he convinced her of his mettle? He sat up.

She rose, and grabbed a robe from the dispenser by the door.

"Wait! You know who I am. Is it given me to know who you are?"

She thought that over, then conceded. "I am Rkizzhi. Pilot. Third Wing." She slithered into the robe and edged carefully out the door without exposing him to public view. It was an act that spoke eloquently.

She had given him her name! She'd not gut him if he tried

to choose her! She'd guarded his privacy. She might even fly with him! Hope exploded into blinding light, a raging warmth. It was several minutes before he had the strength to roll out of the water into the sand. He took his time, then used the facilities for a slow methodical toilet, thinking at warp speed.

He presented himself at Falstaff's door, glanced both ways, then gave the signal an imperious jab. The door slid open to reveal Falstaff, bare to the waist, a towel around his neck, head hair dripping water onto his chest hair. At least he wasn't reeking now, or, Indiw thought, his own senses had mellowed as his tension had drained away.

At Falstaff's gestured invitation, he sidled past and strode to the human's monitor to punch up the record on the *Tacoma* mission. There were still no more volunteers. "Here's how we're going to do this," Indiw said, working the controls. "This is a kind of—oh—bulletin board—just for the business of *Katular*'s Third Wing. Since I'm not Third Wing, I can't cruise the entries to see what they're discussing, but this I can do."

With the human leaning over his shoulder, he explained each move as he spoke the commands to copy the entry from the mission listing. He let the deleted entries show on the screen in the symbols that indicated they had been deleted. "These pilots are First Wing." And then he had to explain that they had backed out earlier that day.

"Why would they do that—volunteer and then back out?"

Indiw had forgotten that Falstaff didn't know about the Interview. "Essentially, it's because they didn't want to fly with me."

"I don't understand. Why did they volunteer in the first place, if they didn't want to fly with you? Your name is first on the list."

"After they volunteered, they found out I'd flown with Pit

Bull. But for that very reason, Third Wing just may produce the volunteers we need."

"So, because First Wing doesn't want to fly with someone who's flown with humans, Third Wing will volunteer to fly with you?"

"No! They'll volunteer to fly with *you*!"

"What makes you think that?"

"Call it a hunch." Indiw had heard that phrase in a human entertainment video he'd been required to study. He hadn't understood the story at all, but he'd become enchanted with the concept of the hunch.

He was astonished though, when Falstaff accepted the phrase as an explanation. The human pulled a seat up beside him and sat studying the screen.

Indiw set up a blank space, invoked the common Tier script, then shoved the control board toward the human. "Put there in your own words why we—you and I—should fly this mission."

"I wouldn't know what to say."

He couldn't tell him that it didn't matter. Whatever he put it would sound alien, bizarre, intriguing, a "unique" experience. He chuckled mischievously. "Say something about why I should be an escort for the bodies. Then sign it."

The human favored him with a wary alertness. "I guess your walk did you some good."

He doesn't know he's being rude. Indiw gestured at the monitor encouragingly. With luck, he wouldn't have to teach Falstaff what the word *walk* meant. He'd be off this ship before he needed to know. *On the other hand, maybe he's figured it out.*

Falstaff addressed the screen. In short order he'd produced five lovely alien sentences that were bound to do the job. "Three brave pilots of your sister ship *Katukin* gave their lives in the battle against the swarm that destroyed her. Their bodies lie aboard *Tacoma* given all possible respect, awaiting a party from *Katular.* As the last survivor of *Katukin,* Indiw has fittingly volunteered for this somber mission. I have elected to fly with him because it is only right that one of their own should escort the dead home. If necessary, the two of us will go alone."

"Perfect!" exclaimed Indiw. "I couldn't have thought of that to save my life! Sign it."

"Pilot Commander Walter G. Falstaff, Pit Bull Squadron, Hundred Twentieth Fighter Wing, assigned to the Carrier *F. T. Tacoma.*" He followed it with some serial numbers that were part of every human's identification code.

It was awesome.

As bait, it was perfect.

Indiw took the control board and brought up Rkizzhi's records, scanning quickly for the data he needed. But even on that first cursory inspection, he was impressed.

"Who's that?"

"Just someone I met." He ditched the screen. Then he made up a set of specifications for pilot experience needed for this sortie. "All the pilots with these qualifications will have this message flashing on their monitors the next time they check in."

"Ah. And you wanted to be sure to include your new friend. You think she'll tell all her friends?"

The man was sharp. This could get uncomfortable. "That's the general idea. Put it to them right, they might be interested."

"In flying with *me*?"

"Certainly not with *me*!" He got up and made for the door, very aware of the human's scrutiny.

"Indiw. Don't underestimate yourself."

"Walt. Don't use the word *friend* when you don't know what it means." When the door closed behind him, he experienced an incredible sense of relief. Only then did he think to look both ways to see if anyone had observed him emerging from the human's place.

But there was no one in sight.

Suddenly aware of growing hunger, he took to his own place and hoped nothing more would disturb him today.

That night Indiw slept with a profound depth he rarely experienced, and woke to discover the *Tacoma* mission roster filled. He knew now that he could work his way into the Third Wing. He understood them.

He didn't even take time to eat, but went immediately to Engineering to help with the work on his fighter. He started to mitigate his reputation by apologizing to the helpful engineer for what he'd done to the fighter. Then he pitched in to help finish the repairs. After seeing what Indiw could do with circuitry, the engineer offered renewed respect and confidence. Indiw basked in acceptance.

Falstaff found him there some hours later as they were just finishing up. "My God, man, I'd no idea where you'd gotten to! Do you realize we've got twelve volunteers to make this trip?"

"Yes, so we'd better be ready." Indiw stood wiping circuit-packing gel from his hands, wondering where else the human had thought he might be. "Come on, I'll give you a hand with your work."

Falstaff was shocked to discover that he was expected to work on his craft himself. Indiw was shocked to find he was so inexperienced despite his theoretical knowledge. But the engineers had been working constantly on the human's fighter, and there wasn't too much left to do. All Tier ships used interchangeable parts and common designs, so the rebuilding of whole systems in the human's fighter was just routine. Between the two of them and the experts, the job was done ahead of schedule.

The only insurmountable problem was Falstaff's paint job. Ardr craft showed polished metal and a few discreet identification markings as adjunct to the automatic transponders they carried. But the human fighters decorated their craft all over. Humans were very visually oriented, especially the males.

Several of the skin panels of Falstaff's craft had been replaced with shiny new ones. On the adjacent plates, the paint was scorched and blurred. Falstaff tilted back the spectrum goggles he wore under ship's lighting and surveyed the patchy effect, face working through several expressions and settling into amusement. "Well, it'll do. Everything else is top notch." He consulted a clock display at the center of the repair hangar. "Besides, it must be about time for the mission briefing. Who's giving it? Where do we go? I want to get a shower—"

"Uh, there isn't going to be a briefing. Each flyer is responsible for learning the parameters of the job and deciding how to approach the problems—independently. Come on, I'll show you how it's done."

With a gesture of gratitude to the engineers, Indiw led off toward the pilot's residence deck. Falstaff caught up with him, again chewing his lower lip but not commenting. Indiw well remembered his own distaste at attending a human mission briefing. He asked, "What are you thinking?"

"It seems like a very wasteful procedure, and what if you all come up with different ideas?"

"I thought I explained. We only fly with people who can look at the same data and come up with the same solutions, all at the same time." *Ideally.* He didn't point out how rarely that happened with a large group like a whole wing.

"But you don't even know these people—I certainly won't think like them."

"I've gained a pretty good notion of how they do things. I think I can explain it to you."

And he tried. He did try. But it was hopeless. When Indiw brought up the Intelligence reports of swarm movements and began reasoning out their course between here and *Tacoma,* Falstaff got lost. It wasn't that he didn't know how to digest such data, it was that whatever his mind did with it, Indiw couldn't follow. The course Falstaff would have set would have left him out in space all alone. None of the Third Wing would go that way.

When they just had minutes to get ready to leave, Indiw said, "All right, forget all that. Do you think you can stick with me? Whatever I do, you stay right on my tail, just beyond shield overlap, as if tied there by a cord?"

They were in Falstaff's place, using his monitor. Everything had been cleaned up and small bags packed. Falstaff was dressed in his own flight suit, and Indiw had requisitioned a new one for himself. He'd chosen a dim green, the color of ocean corral, with metallic threads gleaming at knees and elbows. And it had the extra pockets he'd always wanted. Better yet, it fit like crazy, and he knew the females flying with them would notice.

He watched Falstaff mulling over his question. He liked how Falstaff always thought hard before giving his word on anything.

Eventually, Falstaff nodded cautiously. "I think so."

"I'll stay on your channel and give you plenty of warning on each turn until you get the hang of it. You do understand that we're not going to stay in the same relative position to other craft for more than a few moments at a time? We're not going to present a predictable target to any incoming enemy."

"I understand the theory, I'm just not sure of the practice. Every time I've tried it on the simulator, I've crashed into some Ardr craft. Eventually, I decided you fly at random, and gave up."

Indiw was glad he hadn't eaten recently. He tried not to

look as horrified as he felt. At least Falstaff *had* tried to fly Ardr style on simulator. "If you can stick with me, you won't have a problem."

"But you've never flown with these people before."

"They know that. They'll give me a chance to pick up their style. It's not a difficult one."

Falstaff grinned. "You mean this is a tryout? You're going to join the Third Wing here?"

"I haven't decided yet. We'd better go."

CHAPTER
FOUR
★

THEY FOUND ALL FOURTEEN CRAFT ASSEMBLED IN THE launch bay. There was a large, well-armed cargo transport in the midst of the group of thirteen fighters. Handlers were loading the cargo transport with record cases and shipping containers. Someone had decided to take advantage of the flight to transfer matériel to *Tacoma*. In addition there were crates containing a day's necessities for the pilots, and others holding supplies for any Ardr who might be trapped on *Tacoma* in the future.

The last pilot to sign on had contacted *Tacoma* and arranged for them to stay over to rest for the return, which would be even longer than the journey out since the ships had now begun separating.

The pilots had already started to assemble, and Rkizzhi was checking out the cargo transport. As Indiw approached with Falstaff, the normal chatter stopped and everyone gathered to look the human over. Then eyes turned to Indiw, and he knew his testing was about to begin. He could only hope he had the right answers.

Rkizzhi asked Indiw, "You're going to tow him?"

"Like a trainee."

"You think he can do it?"

"I intend to live a long while, so I'm never absolutely sure of anything. But he's as good as any trainee. Better. He can already fly."

Someone asked, "What if we meet swarm?"

"I'll follow Falstaff. We'll work perimeter on the high-low option I've noticed you use a lot. I'll be sure he doesn't get in the way."

"He knows options?"

"He learns fast."

"You've thought of everything." It was a male voice from the back of the group.

"Can anyone, ever?" He told them the course he'd selected. "It's the best chance for avoiding contact."

Without challenging that, the group broke into small muttering groups. After milling about for a few minutes, the pilots all went to their craft, completing last-minute checks and climbing in. Indiw stood still, watching until he was sure he hadn't lost anyone.

Falstaff asked, "Does that mean they're accepting your choice of course?"

Indiw sighed. "No, it means I picked the same one they all picked." Before he'd been marooned on the human ship, he used to think humans were only subtly different, a difference that made no difference. That they were just people. Now, he knew better. "They're all willing to fly with me—for the novelty of flying with you—but they're willing because I came up with acceptable answers. Let's go."

With one more searching glance around at the other pilots, Falstaff claimed his patchwork craft and disappeared under the canopy.

Indiw climbed aboard his own flyer and secured his little travel bag. The systems were still hot from the last time he'd pulled them on line for a final check. He ran diagnostics again, looking for the slightest hesitation or abnormality, and found none.

He made contact with launch control and had Falstaff moved

into position right behind him. They launched last, out the tunnel through the carrier's energy shields and bursting into clean, black space dotted with bright-colored stars and smearing hazes of nebulas and gas clouds.

The others had gone on, moving slowly enough for them to catch up. That disoriented Falstaff who'd expected to find them nearby waiting, and Indiw said, "Just fall in behind me, and follow. Here's the kind of turn this wing uses for a basic curve left. Stay with me."

He did one in the plane they were traveling in, then executed the training sequence both above and below the plane of reference. Then he did a sequence to the right. Falstaff stuck as if tied on by a cable. By that time, they'd caught up with the others who had established their movements around the less maneuverable cargo ship.

They were keeping it slow and clean, completely basic, giving Indiw all the chance anyone should need to pick up on their style. He fitted himself into the ballet, muttering to Falstaff on the human's channel, sending Falstaff's onboard system the cue signals they'd arranged during the training maneuvers. Meanwhile, he switched off to exchange reassuring comments with the Third Wing pilots, always mindful of his unwanted reputation.

But as time passed, he realized he had indeed found an adequate slot for himself. It wouldn't be anything like *Katukin*, but he could prosper and retire to his own land on Sinaha.

Within three hours, he had walked Falstaff through all the basic maneuvers, teaching all the cues to the human's onboard system, while at the same time admiring the Third Wing pilots. They were artists. It showed in the clean precision of their basics, in the flawless technical perfection of their flying, and in their voices as they criticized one another's performances.

Perfect wasn't good enough for them, yet they weren't tensed up about the flaws they found. They were playing, enjoying finding something to improve, no matter how elementary.

But so far, no one had offered him even one word of criticism. He wasn't accepted here. He and his tow were regarded as cargo, fascinating and unique cargo. Every one of them kept at least one eye on Falstaff's movements, one alert, untrusting eye. And that additional dimension of alertness was adding spice to their game.

Indiw wiped his hands, hitched himself around, adjusted his seat, adjusted his helmet, and went to Falstaff's channel. "Are you ready now to try the real thing?"

"You mean this isn't?"

"No, this is just school figures, taken from less than half their repertoire. They're getting a little anxious because we're approaching the danger zone. It's time to go to improvisation, if you think you can handle it."

"Lord, Indiw, I've still no idea what the hell is going on here."

"Think you can stick with me?"

"What do I do if I lose you?"

"Slow and wait for me to pick you up."

"It sounds so simple."

"If Hyos show up, go to the nearest edge of the maneuvering territory and work there until I find you. Does that sound too hard?"

"Not in theory. All right, but just don't forget I'm back here!"

"You're tied on like a trailer!" He switched to the Ardr channel, adopted a confident tone, identified himself, and said, "I've got it now. Break when ready."

Right on the beat he'd chosen, the pattern broke and shifted and broke again. He heard Falstaff gasp. He told him, "Don't tense up. We've hours to go yet. Besides, they're still keeping it easy. I know what I'm doing. Just follow me."

He was conscious of how clumsy he looked, towing his

tail through the pattern, but he did make the first weave, then the second. He felt Falstaff easing up when he'd proved he wasn't going to crash them into anyone. By this time, Falstaff's onboard could invoke the elementary maneuvers and his facility with combining the basics was improving.

Confidence growing, Indiw tried one of his favorite improvisations, and managed to keep both himself and Falstaff from so much as brushing shields with the other fighters.

Rkizzhi's voice interpolated a word of praise for his work. Others made suggestions for managing his tow. Someone actually commented to Falstaff on the human channel, "I never thought a human could fly that well."

He laughed and replied, "I can't. Indiw's doing all the work. Sorry, fellas, but I gotta concentrate."

The human was doing so well that Indiw added a couple more twists and turns to his next weave, listening carefully for the warning ping his instruments would produce to tell him Falstaff was out of position. It had been a constant sound at first, but now he seldom heard it. In fact, gradually, he'd come to expect its silence.

They made several more weaves across the maneuvering territory, Indiw relaxing more and more into the rhythm of it. He began to feel as if he were really flying a mission. And then, for the briefest instant, as he ran a routine instrument check, he forgot he was towing Falstaff and just moved with the pattern in a turn-and-twist he hadn't taught the human.

But the ping never sounded, and when he looked Falstaff was right on his tail. He heaved a sigh, muttered on Falstaff's channel "Sorry," and finished his instrument check, worrying over a faint haze that wasn't quite a signal.

"You oughta be. That was a dirty trick."

"Consider it a test. You passed." He couldn't clear the haze off his long-range scanner by tuning it, and wondered if one of the new components was deteriorating.

Falstaff muttered absently, "Only because I figured you were going to do something like that."

"You did?" It was a whisper of awe, delight, amazement.

"Don't get carried away, though." There were clicks and tings as Falstaff worked his instruments.

Indiw paused to work out a translation of Falstaff's use of the Tier common idiom. "Don't worry. I won't get carried away. Have you checked your fuel lately?"

"No problem, but this method of flying sure eats fuel."

Indiw refrained from pointing out that good technique could narrow the gap between methods considerably. "I'm doing fine, too, so I doubt we'll need the tanker *Tacoma* has on standby." *Not even if this haze turns out to be Hyos.*

From the leading edge of their maneuvering territory, a male said, "In the midst of having such fun, has anyone checked for Hyos blips?"

Someone in the rear replied, "My scanner keeps ghosting when I take perimeter. There might be something out there."

Indiw said, "I'm getting the same effect. Falstaff, you getting any readings?"

"I thought it was my new circuits needing calibrating. But there could be something out there."

Several others reported similar aberrations. But even as they all examined their calibrations, the wispy ghost images strengthened and the consensus was they had a problem. The pattern broke into battle maneuvers.

Falstaff's appalled voice exclaimed, "My God, what are they *doing?* Indiw!"

Indiw snapped out a string of rapid instructions as his hands and feet coordinated to roll his craft into the newly improvised defensive pattern. "Falstaff, we're going to the perimeter. Stick with me now."

Rkizzhi veered the cargo ship away from the approaching Hyos, and all the other flyers followed suit, weaving their sphere of protection about the slower ship.

Falstaff saw the Hyos first and gave the warning in Tier standard terminology on the Ardr channel.

Then they went sublight, not risking running into Hyos nets and getting dragged down. Suddenly they were in the battle.

There were only five Hyos fighters, perhaps an advance party for some swarm, or maybe survivors of a recent battle. Indiw picked one out, cut it off from its fellows well outside the maneuvering territory, and told Falstaff, "That one's ours. Your turn to lead, Pit Bull Three. Just don't let him push us into friendly fire."

It was a hard fight. The Hyos swooped and dodged and delivered resounding blows with their impulse cannons. At one point, a Hyos missile streaked toward Falstaff's tail. Falstaff dodged, and Indiw got the missile, but the Hyos matched Indiw's maneuver and pounded his shields until Indiw's vision blurred with the vibration.

Falstaff returned, slamming the Hyos with his cannon, but it didn't do any good. Indiw twisted free and dove under the two, stealing a split second to check the auto-scanners for other Hyos. He couldn't believe there were only five of them. But there were no other distant blips.

He acquired the Hyos again just as the Hyos locked on to Falstaff. Falstaff used the mirror image of the maneuver Indiw had just executed, leaving Indiw room to slide right up under the Hyos and pound away at his shields, once, twice, three times.

Then Falstaff came about and fell in above the Hyos, his cannon firing in cadence with Indiw's, setting the Hyos's shields to ringing and rippling up through the spectrum.

In the split instant before the Hyos exploded, he and Falstaff peeled off and got out of the way. Falstaff fell in on his tail as they turned and headed back for the others, exchanging status reports.

The seething ballet of death had subsided. There were no more Hyos. Rkizzhi's voice started the check-in, and Indiw answered for himself and Falstaff, "One kill. No damage. No further sightings. Fuel sufficient to make *Tacoma*."

Even the cargo ship had taken no damage. After the last two disastrous battles, it was a heady feeling for Indiw. But they discussed the mystery of five stray Hyos all the way to *Tacoma*, more interested in Falstaff's theories and his reasons for them than in Indiw's. Indiw was relieved. They were beginning to consider accepting him.

Indiw, emerging into what the humans called the point position, spotted *Tacoma* first and initiated contact with the landing bay commander, identifying the approaching craft, adding impulsively, "And Pit Bull Three and Four returning to base, mission complete."

"I don't have a Pit Bull Four transponder," said *Tacoma*.

Falstaff came on, explaining with a grin in his voice, "This is Pit Bull Three. Pit Bull Four is the Ardr Pilot Commander Indiw, now showing *Katular* ID." He reeled off Indiw's non-winged code.

Accepting Falstaff's word, the voice of *Tacoma* gave them landing instructions via the Tier protocols common to all three of the species of the alliance. A corridor opened in the carrier's formidable defensive shields leading them into the landing bay where the crash fields were deployed, glowing at full strength.

It wasn't an insult. Tier procedures called for treating any incoming craft not based on a carrier as a potential crash landing.

The Ardr followed the Tier procedures, too, standing off the approach corridor and sending in one craft at a time, waiting until the voice of *Tacoma* gave them the all clear for the next one. It was clumsy and slow, but the method had been worked out following a series of accidents due to misunderstandings.

With a careful eye on their fuel gauges, they went in using the same order in which they'd launched. Indiw yielded his place to Falstaff who had tapped his last reserves long before Indiw had. When Indiw glided to a gentle stop in the nest of momentum absorbing fields, his gauges had been showing empty for ten minutes. But he made it.

When he had cracked the canopy, tugged off his helmet, donned goggles, grabbed his bag, and pulled himself out of the cockpit onto the scaffold, Falstaff was there, hands on hips, grinning from ear to ear. Behind him stood a row of humans in dress uniform, with white gloves, shoes, and hats, braced to attention, holding banners and musical instruments on which they blatted out a ghastly noise.

To one side of that line of humans stood Pilot Commander Marla Chancy in a soiled and scorched flight suit, helmet tucked under one arm.

Under that racket, Falstaff accused Indiw, "You knew about this and never breathed a word to me! Deadpan the whole way. How could you!"

From that Indiw surmised this wasn't the way they normally greeted a funeral party. He climbed down close enough to say, "I don't understand. What are they doing?"

Behind the formal reception party, the Ardr pilots had gathered to watch the spectacle.

"As soon as we've been debriefed, we're to report to the main mess to receive the Croninwet Star! We've won the Croninwet, and you knew and you didn't tell me."

The *hero* proclamation! Intent on the flight, Indiw had forgotten. "Walt, I've got to talk to you," he said urgently, trying to steer Falstaff away from the crowd.

But three smartly dressed, ultra-polite security officers came to escort them to their debriefing, handing Falstaff a glowing slate. As he followed Falstaff and their escort, Indiw only had time to raise a hand in signal to the Ardr pilots who were

twitching in and out of wary postures as they watched him
being surrounded and swept toward a bank of lift doors. He
could imagine them itching to ask him why he'd announced
himself as Pit Bull Four, wondering if they'd made a horrible
blunder flying with him.

He didn't know himself why he'd done it except that it
seemed right to finish what he'd started. He'd just have to
deal with the Third Wing pilots later.

Chancy followed them. As they waited by the closed lift
doors, she pushed through the escort to Falstaff. Tucking her
helmet between her knees, she grabbed Falstaff's sleeve and
turned him around. He handed Indiw the glowing slate and
put his arms around the pilot.

The woman clutched his sleeves and shook him violently.
"Shit! Dammit! You fucking bastard! We all thought you were
dead! How could you do that to me?"

Apparently oblivious to all the Ardr watching, Falstaff fastened his mouth over hers. Indiw was certain now that Falstaff
was one of the unlimited kind, and he watched with as much
interest as the other Ardr who were too far away to hear
the human whisper in Chancy's ear, "Sorry I wasn't at the
rendezvous point, but something came up. Better late than
never, no?"

She stepped back, hands on hips. "Oh, hell, you know I'm
glad to see you. But if I'd known you were alive I'd never
have done it."

"Done what?"

"Put you up for the Croninwet, you idiot." She scrubbed at
her eyes with the palm of one hand, then liberated her helmet. "Indiw maybe, but not you. You're too full of yourself
already!"

"*You* did that?"

"Well not by myself! There are over fifty people on
Tacoma's committee, you know."

"But you brought up our names."

"I thought you were dead!"

Bewildered, all Indiw could grasp was that the one human on this ship who could be counted as an enemy had indeed found the best way to destroy him—much more subtle than gutting and leaving him to rot in public, and much more effective. It would certainly prevent anyone else from attempting to fly with a human wing.

She punched Falstaff's arm again, then hurried off as if answering a scramble alert. Indiw was very glad he didn't have to deal with human women on a regular basis.

Wondering what the Third Wing pilots made of Chancy, Indiw glanced toward them, but their escort was moving them off toward a distant bank of lifts. He looked at the glowing slate. The slate held "Orders" that assigned quarters to all the visiting Ardr. They weren't scheduled to start back for a good fifteen hours, and so were invited to attend the formal awards ceremony. The humans had arbitrarily chosen both their quarters and their departure time. *Well,* he thought, *I surely have delivered them to a unique experience.*

Already engineers were swarming over the fighters and the cargo ship, removing the mission recorders, sorting the cargo, and moving the craft off the flight deck to the maintenance hangar.

As their escort eased him and Falstaff into a lift, Indiw saw Rkizzhi break away from her escort and pause to squint up at a sign written on a wall. Her quizzical expression was mingled with delight as she pointed it out to one of her companions. Soon they were all ignoring the escort while they pointed and exclaimed over the concept of the printed directional sign.

The lift doors closed on the scene, shutting out the noise. Indiw leaned weakly against the wall feeling completely unfit to face another Interview, and not knowing how to go about refusing the honor Chancy had arranged for them.

Falstaff stepped between their escorts and put his hand to
the lift controls, redirecting the cage. "We've got to clean up
first. It's been a long trip, and we met Hyos on the way."

Eyes widened, and after a brief argument about time, the
escorts took them to the pilot's deck. Falstaff disappeared
through a door. The escort delivered Indiw to the adjacent
room. "You've been assigned here, Pit Bull Four."

He looked around. "But—where are the other Ardr quartered?"

"B-deck, aft. Engineering built a habitat down there for
them. But you're Pit Bull. You're entitled to better."

They must have heard how I announced myself.

The door opened. It was a small, ugly little compartment
with not a living thing in it. But at least it had facilities—of
a sort. Little water and no sand. The place stank like machinery, and there was the lingering odor of human underneath it
all. He wasn't going to complain though. He slipped through
the door and shut it between himself and the escort. *Only fifteen hours.* Falstaff had endured far more than that without
complaint.

Then he leaned on the door, shaking. The exhilaration of
the flight and the brief but elegant battle drained away. He
still had to face the shambles that was all that was left of his
life. For the last few hours, he'd managed to block all that
out of his mind. Falstaff's performance in space had made it
easy—all too easy—to avoid thinking.

He stripped and made himself use the water devices. To
their credit, the humans had thoughtfully placed little fold-
ers filled with pictorial instructions on each ambiguous item.
There was even a sign on the monitor screen. He changed
into pilot straps and sandals suitable for shipboard use, and
groomed himself as best he could with the items in his bag.

He tried to use the monitor to find out the procedure for
refusing an honor, but had no luck. Then he tried getting a

connection to Falstaff, but an odd signal sounded. At first he thought he'd done something wrong with the system, but after some repetitions he identified the sound as the door signal, not the system complaining at him.

It was Falstaff backed by the escort, dressed so like them, postured so like them, only his scent distinguished him. "Ready? Mustn't keep the brass waiting."

No, I'm not ready! He followed silently, dropping back far enough to notice how Falstaff's stride fell into exact rhythm with the escort. He tried matching his own stride to them. It made his skin crawl. He lagged a little farther, and they waited for him.

Falstaff dropped back and whispered, "Is something wrong?"

"I need to talk to you—privately."

"Look, I'm not really mad at you for not telling me about the Croninwet. You don't have to—"

"No, it's a lot more complicated than that. I have to find out how to refuse this—this whatever it is they want to give me."

"Refu—Indiw, you can't—"

"Why not?"

"Why not! Indiw, the Croninwet has money attached—three years' pay. It's the only decoration that does. It was originated by the Fornak in honor of a human physician who was a hell-uva good pilot, and nobody but nobody has ever refused it."

Indiw stifled a cry of anguish. "But I have to."

"It's never been awarded to an Ardr before. The Fornak would—"

"If I don't get out of this somehow, my whole life will be over."

"What do you mean, your whole life will be over?"

"I'd never be accepted anywhere among Ardr ever again. I can't live with that." He'd said on the record for everyone to see that he chose to decline the humans' honor, but he'd

thought it was some trivial thing of no consequence. He hadn't
known it was a Fornak honor, too.

"Holy shit."

That sounded blasphemous. Maybe he'd got his point across.
Then Indiw thought of what he could do with three years' pay.
It would be wonderful, but it wouldn't get him the land he
needed, and even if it would, the manner of the getting would
make him unacceptable as a neighbor. If he couldn't get out
of this, he'd never, ever, have his own land.

"Relax, Indiw. We'll figure a way around this. But first we
have to get through the debriefing."

Then they were at a labeled door that opened to reveal a
small room with a large screen at one end and a polished
table down the middle. A chair tailored for an Ardr had been
inserted among the others around the table, and even as Indiw
entered, a uniformed person was circling the table removing
glasses of water, cups, and pitchers.

It was an odd deference to Ardr sensibilities. He knew
that humans never sat at a serious conference among equals
without various ceremonial drinks to hand. They knew Ardr
reserved all such functions for strict privacy. It was their ship,
yet they were deferring to him.

He took the chair allotted to him, and examined the controls before him. Other identically clad humans crowded into
the room, one or two bending to ask if he was comfortable.
He assured them he was.

There were fifteen people in the room, plus all of Pit Bull
Squadron, by the time one of them took the end of the table
before the large wall screen and declared his titles by way of
opening ritual. It was the Captain who had first briefed them
before the mission, not the Captain of the whole ship, just
the one who commanded the fighter wings operating from
Tacoma. Glass was his name.

Indiw examined the man carefully. Since flying with the

humans, he'd come to appreciate the concept of "command" on a new level. How could this man live with making all the choices for all those pilots? What kind of person could do that?

After the opening ceremonials, the proceeding was not terribly alien. They showed the recordings of the atmosphere battle over the swarm's nest, and those of the space battle later, though not of their final return from *Katular* or the skirmish on the way. Then they asked questions about what had happened during the battle in the planet's atmosphere, and had Falstaff describe the battle in space.

But these Interviewers had not studied the recordings from Falstaff's and Indiw's fighters as Ardr Interviewers would have. They worked from a quick review of them on the screen combined with their prior study of the recordings Grummon and his wingman had brought back. And none of their questions had anything to do with motivations or personal philosophy or anything important.

The Interviewers focused more on Falstaff than on Indiw, and several times Falstaff was asked questions that should have been directed to Indiw. Falstaff answered, and no one at the table seemed to notice. Indiw let it pass. Half his mind was still worrying about the award and wondering what his enemy would be doing now.

During one lengthy discussion, Indiw noticed Falstaff staring at Grummon who was seated across the table from them.

Falstaff's face seemed chiseled from granite. But the eyes! Indiw would never want to be the recipient of such a gaze.

At length, the Interviewers asked Grummon questions, and Grummon answered for his wingman just as Falstaff had answered for Indiw. Now they closed in on the moment when Grummon had ordered Falstaff abandoned.

There wasn't the slightest change in Falstaff's expression, but Indiw noticed how the human's hand was folded up and poised on his knee under the table. The muscles of that arm strained the fabric of his sleeve. And Indiw thought Falstaff's scent had altered slightly, though that was hard to tell with the whole room reeking of agitated human. But Indiw was sure that physically, if not mentally, Falstaff was ready to kill.

It didn't show in his voice though. He spoke in the exact same cadence as the others, clipped, precise, formal code phrases. The only reaction of the others was in the way their eyes tended to slide away from Grummon now.

Falstaff never said Grummon had done wrong. In fact, he repeatedly asserted the exact opposite.

"Commander Indiw, where did you get the idea for pushing Falstaff's craft like that?"

It took a moment for Indiw to realize the man at the end of the table had spoken to him. "I'm not sure. I had read an engineering article on recent attempts to alter the way impacting energy is absorbed by shields. But I only remembered that afterward. At the time, I was just solving a problem."

"You're an engineer, too?" He searched his notes.

"No. Just a pilot."

"What did your people think of this maneuver?"

"The engineers have banned it. Absolutely."

"Hmmm. Some of our people think it warrants study. But they all agree it was a damnfool stunt. Still, I admire original thinking. And so do the Fornak. You've earned the Croninwet, several times over, for that day's work."

Indiw strove for the same outer calm Falstaff had been displaying, and said nothing.

The Captain dismissed them with an abbreviated ritual and then everyone was on their feet, moving. Not knowing what to do, Indiw followed Falstaff around the table where they intercepted Grummon. Falstaff's fist was still curled tightly in on itself and now his odor was sharp.

Suddenly the fist turned whiter, the jacket sleeve strained tighter, and Falstaff's breath whistled up his nose. Indiw knew he was about to strike. But he remembered it was a major crime for a human to strike a superior officer except on the sparring floor.

Indiw's hand closed over the whitened fist, and he felt the unexpected strength there. "Walt!"

Grummon's eyes focused on Indiw, narrowed.

Someone else came up on Falstaff's other side, took his shoulder, and turned him away from Grummon, speaking urgently.

Grummon said to Indiw, "Can't say I'm sorry to see you two alive. You both did some nice flying out there."

"I thought so," said Indiw, unable to make anything of the melange of scents skirling about the room. But there was a lot of tension and hostility, that was sure. For all he knew, it was just sexual rivalry, and if so, then he wasn't about to undermine Falstaff's position in his pack. "But then we were just shaking down. What we did on the way over here was real flying. Falstaff is one terrific pilot."

"I can't argue that," said Grummon. "And I'm glad you made it."

He turned away then, and the other human let go of Falstaff's shoulder. They turned to watch Grummon march out the door as their breathing evened out.

Within moments Indiw and Falstaff were the only ones left in the room. Falstaff said, "Thanks. I might have done something stupid."

Relieved he'd done the right thing, Indiw said, "Not as stupid as what I've done. I don't know how I'm going to get out of this."

"Oh, yeah, the award." He glanced at a time display. "We only have a few minutes! Come on!"

Indiw followed the human out onto a wide concourse, then

up in a lift, away from the pilot's quarters and the flight decks
and hangars and into what had to be the core region of the
ship. They passed large hatchways standing open onto huge
rooms set with tables or filled with gaming equipment. Every
one of the rooms had people, dressed alike but differently
from others he'd seen, congregated, talking, laughing, jostling
against one another, shouting, or just quietly sitting in rows
watching entertainments.

Then they came to an area where all the people were dressed
more formally again, and they were all working at desks—
huge rooms filled with desks sometimes separated by little
partitions.

"Where are we going?" asked Indiw as they paused at an
intersection.

"Remember, Captain Sutcliff said his door was open to you?
Well, I've been giving it a lot of thought, and it's clear that this
is an instance where it's proper to skip chain of command and
take your problem to the Captain's desk." He skewered Indiw
with a glance and a gesturing finger. "Mind you, there aren't
many of those! Mostly, you'd get your head handed to you
for doing this. But you don't get to command grade without
learning the difference."

"Oh." His "rank" patches had been arbitrarily assigned to
him when they gave him a flight suit and status as a pilot,
and now he realized that each of these symbols represented
years of work, just as his own qualifications did.

"Come on, Indiw, we don't have much time."

They went into a large room with four desks situated behind
a high counter. One of the people got up when Falstaff
approached. Indiw was pretty sure she was a female because
of the way her uniform was cut, though her frontal contours
were not nearly so pronounced as Chancy's. "What can I do
for you, Commander?"

"Ma'am, I'd like to see Captain Sutcliff."

"He's busy preparing for the awards ceremony. Perhaps I can help you?" The female's eyes strayed toward Indiw.

"My partner here needs to talk to him about the awards ceremony. It's important or I wouldn't bother him now. Could you just see if he'll take a moment?"

She began a negative gesture, glanced at Indiw, considered, then ordered one of the men to give the Captain a message. Within a few minutes the messenger was back and deferentially escorting them through another door, and back through corridors and through other doors.

Eventually they found themselves in the largest room Indiw had seen in the working area. It was appointed in the most tasteless combinations of colors, and the furniture was grotesquely oversized even for humans, especially the backs of the chairs.

The man behind the ridiculous desk stood and gestured them to sit in two of the awkward chairs, then settled again, watching his screens. He seemed older than he had at the briefing. His uniform fit his trim figure more loosely, and his upright posture was stiffer, his eyes a brighter black. Sutcliff asked, "Is there something I can help you with, Commanders?"

"My partner here has a problem, and I think you need to hear it from him directly, sir."

Indiw glanced at Falstaff who made a little gesture, then back at the ship's Captain, then said, "I don't know what to say, or how to go about this without giving offense. I've tried to find out, but your ship's system is just too much of a mystery to me. I don't know where to start."

"You've made a good beginning—Indayou? Is that how your name is pronounced?" He lounged back comfortably in his chair, rocking gently, smiling.

Indiw said it for him several times, bemused that the human thought it important enough to try to get it right. Finally, the

Captain said, "Now why don't you try to tell me the problem.
I promise I won't take offense."

Indiw took a deep breath. "I have to decline the award you
have chosen to give me. I have to—"

"What!?" Sutcliff bolted upright, the smile gone. "What do
you mean, decline?"

"He means not accept. He means refuse. He means he
doesn't want the money or the certificate, or anything."

The Captain's eyes flicked to Falstaff who fell silent. Then
Sutcliff skewered Indiw with his dark gaze. "Commander
Indiw, you cannot refuse the Croninwet. It is more than a
military decoration, more than a prize of the battlefield. It is
an honor of the Tier. It is the kind of honor that is most often
given posthumously to widows and orphans. This presentation
will be broadcast to all the Tier worlds. The timing has been
carefully chosen so we can send—"

Indiw pushed into the back of the huge chair wishing he
could close it up around him. *Everywhere?!*

"What is the matter, Commander Indiw?"

"I can't accept—"

The Captain touched a control on his desk and, interrupting
Indiw, ordered someone else to come into the office. "Commander Trilucca is *Tacoma*'s Protocol Officer. Her department
is in charge of our contacts with ships of other species and cultures. Perhaps you can explain to her exactly what the problem
is and we can work something out. Or—we don't have much
time to go through channels—is there someone on *Katular* I
should be discussing this with?"

"No!" It came out too loudly. "No, it is entirely a personal
matter. Private. My reasons are not to be discussed. I have
chosen to refuse."

"Refusing what?" came a lighter voice from behind them.

Falstaff and Indiw rose to greet the woman who came into
the room. When a chair had been drawn near the desk for her

to sit in, Indiw said, "It's simple enough. I have chosen not to go to the awards ceremony."

Trilucca smiled. "That's all right. If it's the ceremony that's bothering you, you don't have to be present to receive the award. We can just—"

"No! I will not accept any award."

Trilucca silenced Sutcliff with a hasty gesture. The power of females among humans must be far greater than textbooks even hinted. She said, "Possibly we're operating on different assumptions. Indiw, listen, and don't interrupt until I'm finished. Then I'll listen to you. Agreed?"

"Agreed."

"By the time Grummon limped back close enough to *Tacoma* to order S&R out for you, it was too late for you. Pilot Commander Chancy tried and nearly died for it. She's absolutely the best S&R has, and even she had to admit you were dead. When Chancy brought Grummon's recordings of your battle to our attention, the way you and Falstaff worked together with Pit Bull against the Hyos who outnumbered you, we knew we'd seen something extraordinary.

"The awards committee here on *Tacoma* sat in executive session with Captain Sutcliff and decided to put you and Falstaff in for all the top awards. There were two or three others you were considered for that you didn't get. But the Croninwet Committee was meeting on Aberdeen—it's only a couple of hours from here, you know—and as soon as they saw those battle sequences, they told us you two would be the next recipients.

"Then came word that you had both survived, and on Captain Sutcliff's query, we learned that you, Indiw, had saved Falstaff by a most unorthodox maneuver. When we informed them, the Croninwet Committee announced the citation to all the Tier worlds and released some of that battle recording along with an account of how you'd saved Commander Falstaff.

"In a few more days, everyone will have seen that announcement. Politicians have already been centering all their major speeches on how the bestowing on an Ardr of a Fornak award heretofore given only to humans strengthens our—always vulnerable—alliance against the Hyos incursions. This is being held up as a symbol of hope for a brighter future. The Fornak are already launching massive public celebrations.

"If you pull out now, it will be taken as a major insult, at least by the Fornak, and there are some humans who don't understand Ardr who would love a chance to cut your people out of the trade alliance. I understand that you personally, for private reasons, would prefer not to be involved. But if you pull out now, some people—even some people in a position of power—will hold your entire species accountable for your conceit."

"But I'm not con—"

She held up a hand again, patting the air. "Yes, I know, *apparent* conceit. But they will see it as real conceit, and a type of conceit typical of *all* Ardr.

"By graciously accepting the award, you can effectively gut all those enemies of the Ardr—all those who do not want the Ardr to prosper and expand so that they can move in on territory the Ardr would otherwise claim. This is economic warfare, a little different from piloting a fighter against the Hyos, but with the same essential objective. And it requires the same essential character traits to triumph in this kind of warfare."

Stunned at the ramifications, Indiw could only say, "But you don't understand. I must decline—"

"Well, then at the very least, you'll have to go out on the platform beside Captain Sutcliff and make a speech rejecting the award. Considering the enemies of the Ardr who will be listening, eager for ammunition to use against your whole people, what could you say in such a speech that would convince all of them you weren't making a gesture of contempt for the most coveted award a pilot can aspire to? And contempt for those who created and bestowed that award?"

"A speech?"

"That will be heard on every Tier world. What could you say?"

Indiw couldn't think of a word he could say, and even if he knew what to say he wasn't at all sure he could get a single word out with so many people listening.

Trilucca added quietly, "And regardless of what you said, Commander Falstaff here would spend the rest of his life answering for your behavior. It'll go down in the history books. They'll make documentaries about it.

"But if you accept the award graciously, in a few years people will have forgotten it ever happened. Battlefield awards are not news. Turned-down battlefield awards *are*. The best way to preserve your privacy is to accept the spotlight for a little while, and become just another award recipient, not the one and only ever to reject the award."

Indiw felt the loss of *Katukin* in that moment as he never had yet. There was no one on *Katular* he knew well enough to ask for a verification of this human's reasoning. The pilots who'd come to *Tacoma* with him were strangers. He didn't have anyone left whose judgment he trusted as his own. Except maybe Falstaff. But the human couldn't possibly comprehend the problem.

And even if he could, it wouldn't be good to discuss the threat that Ardr saw in humanity with a human, and a human hero at that. It would only prove he was the traitor *Katular*'s Interviewers suspected him to be.

Had Trilucca told him the truth? After all, a human female had gotten him into this—through ignorance, stupidity, or malice, he didn't know which. He said, "Would it be possible to see something of this publicity coverage you've spoken of?"

Sutcliff threw his arms in the air and exclaimed, "Well, of *course!* Here, we're getting feed from Aberdeen all the time." He worked a control and behind his desk a large screen appeared, flicking to a scene of hundreds of humans thronging a public square.

The announcer was a Fornak, a familiar voice to any Ardr because this one did many reports in Ardr languages. Now he spoke a standard Tier dialect. It took only a moment for Indiw to be sure he was speaking of his exploits with Falstaff. And a moment later the screen showed the sequence in the air battle where Falstaff saved his life. Then there were bits from the space battle.

All the while, the familiar—and famous—voice spoke in hushed, awed tones of the importance of the Croninwet going to a human/Ardr flying team. "Turn it off!" Indiw dropped his face into his hands, clenching his fingers around his horns for a moment, oblivious to those watching him.

If he refused the award, his battlefield would expand to encompass three species, two of which he didn't understand, and his battle would spread to all the Tier worlds.

If he accepted, he'd have a battle on the Ardr worlds on terms and conditions he full well understood, and where he could maybe win back respect and a chance at land. Maybe. Even though he couldn't see any way to win right now, he'd learned one thing as a hatchling. In any competition, it wasn't over until you were dead and eaten.

He told Trilucca, "I had no idea matters had gone so far, or that anyone would be interested in some completely routine flying by an unimportant pilot. I choose to accept the award. I'll deal with the personal difficulties—later."

"I do admire your fortitude," said Trilucca. Adopting an adequate imitation of a respect posture, she added a formal benediction that was, under the circumstances, completely inappropriate. "You will surely defend your land well." She stood and with the Captain's permission left.

Indiw didn't notice, and he didn't see Falstaff rise, picking up some subtle signal from the Captain. All he could think of was that a few short days ago when he'd left *Katukin* to fly a routine mission against a swarm, life had been full of hope. Now there was nothing. He had absolutely nothing left, not even the credibility his record had earned him. Even he wouldn't choose such a disgraced one for a neighbor.

" . . . let the Captain get on with his job. Indiw?"

Indiw rose and let Falstaff guide him through the maze of human public spaces to the cramped compartment he'd been ordered to occupy. It suddenly seemed fitting that even choice of abode was stripped from him. Falstaff talked with energetic enthusiasm the whole way, but Indiw didn't hear a bit of it.

He came to full alertness only when he opened the door to his quarters and the odor hit him. "Someone's been in here!" He backed away from the door, hand and toe claws flexing even though he knew the person had gone. It was the ultimate violation. Despite everything, something inside him did not accept that as his due.

Falstaff looked through the open door bewildered. "How can you tell?"

Exasperated, Indiw charged through the door tracking the fresh smell of human. And there on the padded platform that was supposed to be a bed he found—*things*. He picked up the foreign objects and vented his sudden rage by throwing them at the open door—and at Falstaff who had politely remained beyond the vacuum seal cowling. With each object, Indiw screamed a curse at the absent intruder.

The human dodged the heavy items, then became tangled in lengths of fabric. He caught the last heavy case and parried Indiw's move to close the door in a futile attempt to shut out the reek of human. "When you calm down come to 1208-B and we'll talk." He piled the *things* outside the door and then let it close.

Indiw paced and raged and slashed at the walls until his throat hurt and his claws had dulled. He needed to kill someone, preferably the intruder. It was a pure primal need and had nothing to do with proper conduct.

But it wasn't just the intruder. He'd been so secure in his position in his wing on *Katukin*. And now—*now!* He didn't even have a place to sleep! And things would get worse, much worse, from now on. Who would choose to fly with a disgraced pilot?

After a while he found some shreds of discipline and dignity. With a tremendous effort of will, he turned his purely instinctive random rage toward the honed and deliberate movements of combat practice. Modified for the confined space, it was doubly intense, doubly effective.

Gradually his breathing calmed, his mind cleared, and he was relieved he had not actually killed anyone. Someday, when he held his own land, he'd have the unquestioned right to kill intruders. He had not yet earned that right.

True, no Ardr would have blamed him, had he surprised the intruder in the act and killed in sheer reflex. But it would have been embarrassing to have killed a human for behaving in a human fashion in a human environment. And he had enough trouble without trivia like that to distract him.

And, yes, there was still a chance he could recoup his reputation. There had to be a chance, but certainly not if he went around killing people he did not yet have a right to kill. Even if he couldn't see it at the moment, there still had to be a way for him to qualify as a landholder.

He was aware he was telling himself that, over and over, phrased in different ways. He was also aware that he didn't believe it yet, not deep down in his gut where it counted the most. But maybe, if he kept telling himself firmly enough, he'd come to believe it, and then he could do something to make it true.

But first, first he had to get through this ordeal his one human enemy had inflicted on him. If he didn't think about the hero label and instead concentrated on doing this as the defense of land, for his neighbors and for himself, he might not disgrace himself too badly.

And when it was all over and he'd somehow won through to become landed, and maybe powerful in the affairs of a planet, he would have a most valuable lesson to guide him—never, ever make an enemy of a human, but especially not a female human.

He brought his movements to a controlled close and stood panting in the cramped space. With an effort, he convinced himself he had to examine the *things* he'd evicted. He opened the door, looked up and down the deserted hall, and kicked the pile into the room.

There was a Pit Bull uniform cut to fit him, complete with boots, and lined with a soft material that would buff his hide rather than abrade it. It was a different color and style than any they'd given him before, but it had all the appropriate tags and patches. Several small cases with *Katular* labels contained grooming items, prepared rations, and a basic pharmacy. Those smelled of Rkizzhi's handling—and she hadn't been well disposed toward him at the time she'd handled them. They must have come from the cargo they had brought.

There was even a room-sized scent eradicator. He seized on it and activated it, opening the door to the small facilities room and carrying the spewing packet into every corner of the place. He was sneezing and coughing by the time he finished, but it was worth it.

Among the *Katular* containers, he found one from *Tacoma*

filled with data nodules: Welcome to *Tacoma*, Rules and Regulations Aboard *Tacoma*, Customs and Practices Aboard *Tacoma*, Daily Procedures Aboard *Tacoma*, Orders for Pilot Commander Indiw, Pit Bull Four. He seized that one and discarded the rest unexamined.

He wanted to flush it down the toilet but it would probably block it up. He could visualize the place knee deep in human waste. He could almost smell it.

No, he'd find a better way. He hurled it at a wall, and dropped into the oddly *wrong* chair. He had chosen, and now he had to do what he'd chosen to do and follow that path wherever it led. Behaving like an adolescent victim of his own hormones would not earn him any land.

Half an hour later, his room in perfect order, he presented himself in Pit Bull uniform before the door that had 1208-B written on it in bright figures, and even more brightly sported Falstaff's scent strewn across the door's surface in no particular pattern. On the wall beside the door a sliding plate held the name Falstaff. The holder beside his own door had been empty.

The door slid open at his signal to expose Falstaff, holding a lit reading slate, uniformed just as Indiw was, facing another man in a different uniform. The compartment was just as cramped as Indiw's was, but Falstaff didn't let him retreat. "Come in, Indiw. You have a decision to make."

Jaws clenched, claws carefully controlled, Indiw stepped just inside and let the door shut behind him, striving to identify a familiar odor. He averted his gaze from the other males, and turned his back politely to show them how his muscles bunched in anticipation of a challenge because they were all crowded into too small a space.

Falstaff moved around the one who was standing ramrod straight. "This is the Yeoman who put those things in your quarters."

Ah! That's the odor! The deodorant had temporarily killed his nose.

"I've instructed him on his error," continued Falstaff. "It's for you, Commander Indiw, to define his penalty."

Indiw choked down a resurgence of his primitive rage. Why had Falstaff tempted him with the one he so desperately needed to kill and must not? Cruelty?

"Indiw? What penalty do you choose for him?"

"Penalty?" Surely not cruelty. It wasn't Falstaff's style.

"Yes. He knew it was your quarters, but he failed to look up Ardr protocols."

Indiw could scarce believe it. Falstaff was imposing Ardr protocols on a fellow human to spare Indiw's sensibilities. "What are the appropriate penalties for such an oversight?"

"Varying periods of extra duty, and/or mastering protocol texts and proving it on computer testing."

"I believe he should master the protocols for both Ardr and Fornak visitors, and do four hours extra duty every day for twenty workdays."

"You heard him, Yeoman."

"Yes, sir! Thank you, sir!"

"Dismissed."

Stiffly the Yeoman sidled past Indiw and was gone.

Indiw watched the door close. "I don't understand. Should he not have chosen the penalty for himself?"

"That's not the way we do things. Besides, you'd have preferred to gut him, and in a way you just did. Twenty days with no social life!"

"I was unreasonable?"

"Oh, no, not at all. He certainly won't make that mistake again, and boy will he have a story to tell his grandchildren!"

In a wild flash Indiw saw the Yeoman as an old man sitting with small humans all around him, knowing for a fact that these were the product of his own loins and thus feeling a need to prevent them from coming to harm. He shuddered, skin rippling under the soft cloth lining his clothing. Such an alien concept! But it must account for many of the bizarre practices among humans if only one could twist the mind around the idea.

"Do you have children?" he suddenly asked Falstaff.

The human gave him such a look he stepped back and gestured apology. "I should not have asked."

"You didn't have to ask. You could have looked it up. It's in my file. My wife and son were killed by a swarm that broke through and got the passenger liner they were traveling on. My brother died fighting that same swarm. His wife and children are my nearest kin. They're living on Aberdeen. I send those kids birthday presents. I go to their home when I get leave, and I take those kids hunting and fishing. Does that answer your question?"

"Generously." Actually, it only raised more, but he'd already overstepped the bounds. Hunting and fishing? On the land of his brother's wife? In a pack with her children? None of the pack hunters evolved on the Ardr homeworld would even recognize their own children any more than any Ardr would. Until you thought about it, it almost sounded like humans had something in common with Ardr—going home to hunt and fish.

"Good," said Falstaff, dismissing the subject while waving the slate in his hand. He interrupted himself. "Did you see this? Indiw, I can't thank you enough for stopping me from decking Grummon! That would have been the biggest mistake of my career."

Indiw took the slate and looked at the screen. The defined area was labeled as Falstaff's orders, but Grummon's name was highlighted. He understood only that Grummon had left *Tacoma* with his wingman, and Falstaff would be, as of tomorrow, Pit Bull One with Indiw assigned to the Pit Bull Two slot. The other two positions in the squadron were empty, and Falstaff was to make recommendations.

And I got myself into this by announcing myself as Pit Bull Four.

★
CHAPTER
FIVE
★

"IT'S A PROMOTION, INDIW, AND I'D'VE BLOWN IT IF YOU hadn't held me back."

"Didn't take much holding. You have remarkable control." *Better than mine!*

The human cocked his head to one side. "What would you have done if I'd jumped him?"

"Put my claws to his throat and subdued him so you'd no longer feel the immediate need to destroy him."

"Jesus! It's a good thing I didn't hit him." His gaze raked across the time display on his desk screen. "Let's get out of here. We can't be late for this!"

When they arrived at the awards ceremony, all the others had already assembled in the large public space normally used for eating in groups.

Crews operated professional recording equipment in two corners of the room, with another station up on a platform suspended high over the big double doors. At the far end away from the door, lights burned down on a raised area. Indiw discerned the telltale traces of sound pickup fields surrounding the area under bright lights.

Row upon row of chairs facing the light were filled with neatly uniformed humans all turning this way and that, talking with others. The human scents were overpowered by the stale odor of cooked food, and that was in turn swamped by the reek of freshly cooking food. Indiw was glad he hadn't eaten.

As Falstaff led the way toward the lighted area, he muttered through a fixed smile, "Lord, I'm starved, that smells so good, and this is going to last for hours."

Then they were edging into the cramped space behind a curtain at one side of the lighted area. They stood a moment amid poles and banners, strange uniforms, people waving lighted slates and shouting directions. Standing on a chair presiding over it all was Trilucca.

"*There* you are at last," she said to them as they came through the curtain. "You belong in that corner. The Admiral will lead you out. And, ah, Indiw, with the lights down so low, do you really need those goggles? We've tried to adjust the lighting for you."

"Yes!" he blurted, and then regretted his rudeness. They were doing their best. But he had to be able to see if any of the Third Wing showed up to watch his disgrace in person. "Uh—the contrast between the stage and the rest of the room is—a bit harsh."

"Oh. Well." Trilucca made a notation.

Falstaff stuffed the two of them into the back rear corner of the waiting area, obviously trying to give Indiw a proper breathing space. But with all the people churning about, it was impossible. They kept pushing Falstaff into Indiw. "Sorry, Indiw."

"It's all right," he answered. "But I knew we'd be too early."

"No. They had to hold up waiting for us. It's past starting time now."

That had been Indiw's point. Nothing had started yet, so why were they here? But the humans seemed to be enjoying the process of working themselves into a nervous sweat. Maybe it was part of the ceremony? At least they did it with enthusiasm, telling each other how many people on how many worlds would be listening or getting this on recordings and how crucial it was that they do everything just right so all their relatives would be proud of them. He hoped it wasn't important for him to participate because it all meant nothing to him.

Then, after what seemed a long interval in the increasingly stuffy air, suddenly the musicians sorted themselves out from the crush, formed two lines, and marched into the lighted area where they produced a loud sound. In the ensuing silence, a woman's voice called, "Attention!"

A concerted crackle-snap-scuffle heralded the unison movement of the audience. Then another large group of uniforms assembled, deployed banners, and slowly stepped out into the light.

At last Indiw was allowed room to stand free. Before he could really enjoy it, the hall filled with noise. It went on for a long time before Indiw recognized the cadence as singing. Even Falstaff was doing it, standing stiff and holding a salute. Indiw realized he'd heard that song before, but it sounded different when you were standing in the midst of the noise. It was a large pack's ceremonial rallying cry.

And then everyone out there was sitting, the lights dimmed, and someone narrated a showing of the battle sequences for which the honors would be bestowed, this time including Indiw's own flight recorder's images of his nudging Falstaff's nearly derelict fighter. It had been heavily edited.

Meanwhile, Sutcliff, Glass, and a woman wearing an Admiral's uniform came through a back door. Indiw recognized her from endless appearances on the news. At her approach, Falstaff stiffened. The Admiral gestured, but Falstaff barely eased his stance. After all, she was female, and looked formidable enough to gut them all without disarranging her hair.

Trilucca came over consulting her slate, her face lit from below by the screen. In a whisper she gave orders to the Admiral, which confirmed Indiw's opinion of her power among humans. "All right, Admiral Damien, you'll walk straight out to the podium. Indiw, Falstaff, you follow and stand about halfway between the curtain and the podium and wait for the Admiral to call you forward. When she's finished presenting, each of you should step up to the podium and say a short thank you—don't make a long speech, please."

Indiw made a negative movement, and remarkably Trilucca caught the meaning. "A problem, Commander?"

"I will say nothing."

The Admiral said, "It's customary to express gratitude in this circumstance, even when we don't feel it at the moment— and truthfully, most people can't feel anything but terrified while facing billions of people hanging on their every word!"

"Uh," said Falstaff, "with your permission, Admiral, I think it might be better if I just said something like, 'On behalf of both of us, I'd like to ask for a moment of silence for the brave men and women who died during the battle that now brings us such honor.' "

"That's good!" said Trilucca, writing on her slate.

Falstaff looked at Indiw and closed one of his eyes. Knowing how sensitive human eyes were, Indiw was concerned. But the pain evidently passed quickly.

And then they were being pulled into position behind the Admiral who was preceded by the two Captains carrying large, flat, polished boxes. Indiw took station at Falstaff's shoulder and determined to stay there and not think.

Once at the podium, the Admiral talked and talked, but Falstaff stood without moving, no expression on his face, eyes not even flicking about. Indiw managed to mimic the stillness except for the eyes. He had to scan the audience to see if any of the Ardr were here. But of course, they weren't. Still, they were surely watching on the ship's monitors.

Thinking of how they must be feeling soiled by association, he missed his cue to step forward, and so dropped a step behind Falstaff.

It was just as well, for they gave Falstaff his box first, shaking Falstaff's hand with broad, jerky gestures, freezing to pose for a small group of men and women with recorders who were on the floor at the foot of the raised area. These were not in uniform, and some of them were Fornak. Each of them had two or three identification tags dangling from their clothing. It finally dawned on him that these were the representatives of the interstellar news media who traveled with Admiral Damien—whose every move created news enough to fill a day's broadcasts.

Then the Admiral was handing the other box to Indiw. He forced his hand out and made his fingers close over it without extending his claws. Much.

Then he retracted his claws hard, expecting the Admiral to seize his hand as she had Falstaff's, but she took two steps backward and made a creditable attempt to indicate respect with a body movement.

Indiw returned the gesture, trying not to seem as if he were correcting her style.

She relinquished the podium to Falstaff who repeated what he'd planned to say. Somebody out in the dimness rose, and a moment later everyone was standing. It became so silent Indiw fancied he heard the recorders whispering in the back of the hall. The place throbbed with an emotion he couldn't name. Sadness and grief were too pale beside the aching tears those humans were refusing to shed. Laced through the silent scream of loss was a beating pride and a rising will. A pack saluting its fallen. He shuddered.

"At ease."

With that eerie unison move, they sat, but the heady mixture of scents didn't dissipate. Indiw was astonished at how he'd seemed to understand the subtext of that silence.

He was sure he hadn't imagined it. It was too bizarre. He wondered what the other Ardr pilots might have made of that experience had they been present, not that he'd ever have a chance to ask now. Who would speak to him after this?

He had to take a seat behind the podium next to Falstaff while the two Captains spoke. Indiw looked at the polished boots on his feet, flexed his toe claws into the internal cushions, and thought about his life. He'd done it. It was over. It was too late to repair the damage. How was he going to live with it? What could he possibly do now?

Katular was a total lost cause. He could try another ship. Or maybe give up piloting and find another way to earn land. He had no idea what other talent he might have to exploit. He was such a good pilot, he'd never doubted after the initial training missions that he could succeed.

Maybe he *had* been a victim of goralchor. Maybe that was why he'd lost it all. If so, he'd come to his senses now.

All he had left was the money he'd earned as a pilot. And there was the Croninwet money, a nice chunk. But it took more than money to buy land. It took neighbors to accept you, it took deeds acknowledged as worthy, and it took strength of character demonstrated in the way you handled choices—and carried through on the ones you announced.

All his potential neighbors had died with *Katukin,* and his deeds and choices of the last few days pointed to fatal character flaws. There was no one living who could look at his record and not say, "This is a traitor who will hand us over to the humans at his first chance."

As he sat on the stage squinting against the dazzle, facing humans he couldn't quite see, he held his own damnation between his hands in a smooth case the dark reddish color and smooth polished texture of Ardr skin. He knew the case was covered with the hide of a herd herbivore they used as a meat animal. It was far and away the most repulsive thing he'd ever touched in his life.

At long, long last, the humans decided their ceremony was over. As he'd seen them do before, they snapped to their feet, and then broke, just like a fighter wing breaking from one pattern weave to another.

The lights changed, becoming even throughout the hall, and as far as Indiw could see, the patterns the humans wove now really were the chaotic and unpredictable mess that Falstaff had thought a wing's flight patterns were.

Falstaff rose, and a large clump formed around him. Everyone else involved in the ceremony began drifting out of the room while other humans arrived with stacks of tables and noisily rearranged the furniture. As huge double doors opened at the side of the room, the food odor got heavier. It smelled like rotting excrement.

A group of people assembled at the edge of the platform seemed to be watching Indiw. They were deployed on either side of the little staircase that led down to the floor. Indiw glanced to his right. The curtain was gone. There were several groups of people between him and the door through which the Admiral had come earlier.

With his eyes on the people between him and that door, he kept his attention on the ones gathered about the stairs. The moment he saw a path open to the door, he moved. He was out the door, pulling it shut behind him, securing it with a vacuum seal before any of them noticed.

He tucked the case under one arm and looked about. It was a gleaming stainless-steel place lined with racks securing loose tableware. But it had an exit sign glowing above another passageway. He followed some white-clad humans, and eventually found himself in another public corridor.

He had no idea where he was relative to his place and no idea how to find out, except by asking, which he wasn't about to do. He kept moving, trying to seem as if he knew where he was going and was in a moderate hurry. A few humans saluted him, and a few offered broad grins and a hand sign he took for approval. But most just ignored him.

Every time he thought he had found his orientation, he'd turn a corner and discover how wrong he'd been. He was getting very hungry now. He hadn't eaten since the previous day.

He found a sign that said B-deck, and remembered that was where the other Ardr were quartered. He turned the opposite way. That led to a fetid heat with an acrid tang to it. Through huge transparent doors he saw a gigantic depression filled with water. Humans wearing less than he'd ever seen humans wear were churning the water to froth with their frantic activities while rows of spectators cheered.

He backed out hastily, so embarrassed his horns ached. It was just the sort of place he'd expect to find Falstaff and Chancy attending to what they both obviously ached for. But he'd never thought human pack instinct went so deep as this. *Spectators!*

He fled through another corridor, up a service tube, and down in a lift that refused to take the coordinates of the pilot's deck. After that near disaster, he became keenly aware that there must be more kinds of trouble he might get into comparable to what he'd saved Falstaff from on *Katular.* He had to get back to his own place.

Then he spotted open lift doors and dove through them before they closed. "Pilot's deck!" he commanded.

His feet were driven into the flooring, and then the doors snapped open. He blundered out with relief, for this was the first lift that had accepted his command.

Only then did he realize he had made a terrible mistake. He was in some kind of a gym, and it just might be the wrong kind.

It was a huge, open space divided by low walls. At one end

lines were drawn across the room, and at the other movable walls held targets. On the far side, where the targets were close to the marksmen, Pilot Commander Chancy, dressed in a loose white suit, crouched with a simple, primitive device stretched between her hands, leveling a metal-tipped, fletched missile at a target. The target bristled with half a dozen missiles that hadn't hit true.

She had wrapped a black cloth around her eyes, and she was moving in slow circles, clean, disciplined circles such as Masters taught those aspiring to become landed.

Before he could quietly retreat, she let fly, and the missile stood in the center of the target. In one fluid movement, she nocked another missile, spun, and nailed the center of the target again. She had found her center. And she was *good.* Better than Indiw.

The nearly stagnant air finally wafted him her scent. There was a bitter tang—rage? Anger? He was only just beginning to know humans well enough to guess. But obviously she was here working in to center because something had upset her. Very, very stealthily, he retreated into the lift, eyes never leaving the tight, dangerous coil of human female.

If she had been Ardr, he would know that her next move would be to walk. But he had no idea what a human laden with such energies would do.

He made it into the lift unnoticed and jabbed at the controls, not caring where it took him.

It deposited him in a narrow passage, dimly lit and lined with pipes. A maintenance tunnel. He was really lost now but was not going to get back into that lift. He wandered for a long time until he found a door with a brightly lit grill panel. He emerged on a broad hallway, filled with a glowing dazzle. There were large open areas off the hall, each lit and decorated differently. And the entire place smelled of the recreational brews humans favored.

Metabolically, humans shared the use of certain common sugars with Ardr. He was hungry enough to make that idea sound interesting. So he found a shadowed spot in the back of one darkened, deserted establishment that he told himself would be sufficiently private and experimented with the screen built into the table.

The display demanded, "Insert your Orders nodule."

He dropped his face into his hands and squeezed his horns. He was so tired. He stayed that way for a long time.

Someone sat down opposite him. "This seat taken?"

It was Falstaff. He'd left his award somewhere, but he was still dressed formally.

Joy exploded inside Indiw and struck him speechless.

"I got away as fast as I could, Indiw, but you were gone. I've been looking for you for hours. Never thought I'd find you in a closed bar!"

"I wouldn't be here if I knew how to find my quarters." It was the last thing he'd intended to say.

"I know how that feels! That's why I've been looking for you. Are you ready to go?"

Indiw rose. "There's nothing here for me."

Standing, Falstaff paused. "I'm not too sure of that. You in the mood for an adventure?"

"What do you mean?"

Falstaff extracted a nodule from the belt at his waist and passed it through the receptacle in the table. Then he instructed the table's controls. A compartment in the wall beside them opened to reveal a pair of square bottles with colorful labels. Falstaff snagged the necks of the bottles between his fingers and said, "This stuff's hell on an empty stomach. Come on, let's go home."

At the end of the hall they found a lift that took them within a few steps of their doors. So easy, so close, but he hadn't known. "Where do you get a map of this ship?"

"Map's on your Orders nodule. So you'll have it with you at all times."

At Indiw's silent look, Falstaff added, "They gave you one. Didn't they? In the little box full of nodules? Had everything in it you need to know—had better know—to live on this ship. Before you get drunk, I suggest you read the one labeled Emergency Procedures. Very embarrassing for a Commander to run the wrong way in a drill. So don't get too drunk. Since right now the whole ship is celebrating, there's sure to be a drill. They like to interrupt celebrations with a good shock."

"Humans, too?" It was amazing they hadn't had a drill or two while Falstaff was on *Katular*.

Falstaff laughed. Indiw joined him. For all their differences, their similarities were always surprising.

"Here," said Falstaff, putting one of the bottles in Indiw's hand. "But be sure to eat first. Oh, and read the label on that bottle, too. Carefully. Then check out the nodule on emergency drills." He mused, "You know, I never found anything on drills in *Katular*'s system."

"You just choose a station you're most experienced at. Pilots go to the hangars. I showed you how to get there."

Falstaff blanched. "Indiw, seriously, I suggest you read the Emergency Procedures nodule as close as you know how. If you've never seen the like before, don't let boredom drive you away from it. Your life could depend on it. And sleep with your goggles to hand. The lighting changes during an emergency."

Indiw examined the recessed light panels. They didn't seem to be the sort that would draw a lot of power. "Why?"

"Human retinal sensitivity and the properties of light filtered through smoke. They pick the best wavelength for us to see by under the worst conditions."

"Oh. I will take your advice."

"I hope so." The human hit the control to open his own

door, but checked on the threshold looking into the room. "What are *you* doing here?"

"Walt, we have to talk." It was Chancy's voice.

Indiw, left standing alone in the corridor, a bottle in one hand and his polished award case in the other, quickly maneuvered through his own door. Maybe human women weren't so unpredictable after all. It's just that he never expected they'd do it in someone's quarters, not after all that public display. But then maybe he hadn't thought it through. Maybe they hadn't done anything so drastic in public. Which would mean he'd misjudged Falstaff.

Maybe this business with pack forming with relatives required a mating pair to use the territory of one or the other to form the bond? He wished he'd paid more attention to the texts on human behavior, but it had always seemed so distant and boring—and there weren't any general rules. On each planet they colonized, humans developed the most bizarrely divergent customs, even contradictory ones. However, one thing was becoming clear. Mating customs were a whole lot more important in understanding humans than any Ardr text had ever indicated.

He had a squirming feeling that he was on the brink of understanding something crucial about humans that nobody had ever known before. But that was probably just hunger warping his brain chemistry.

He made food his first order of business. It didn't take long. Rations were not meant to be lingered over.

As he ate, he examined the label on the bottle Falstaff had given him. Not enough alcohol to matter, but the other ingredients! It was potent stuff—all properly certified for Ardr consumption. He tasted it. It was—interesting.

Something hit the wall of the adjacent cabin with a thud. Alarmed, he sat up, looking at the spot with horror. It had sounded like a body. But then he'd expected Chancy to be

the violent type. Then her voice screeched, " . . . has Indiw
to do with . . ."

Falstaff's rumble shouted her down. " . . . *told* you . . .
Ardr . . . reported in to *Tacoma* as soon as . . ."

Embarrassed at overhearing such private proceedings, he
went in search of the stray nodule labeled Orders. He found
it on the floor in a corner. Not a good practice, losing track
of small, dense items. In a power failure, *Tacoma* could lose
gravity and send everything flying. The nodule could theoreti-
cally take out an eye.

He rummaged out the nodule case and arranged himself a
place to curl up and read, trying to stay far enough away from
the wall that he wouldn't overhear any more. With the bottle
and a glass set to one side, he divested himself of the irksome
uniform, inserted the first nodule in the receptacle on a slate,
and settled in to study.

The nodules were in Tier standard and also translated into
three Ardr languages. Unfortunately, none of the Ardr languages were among Indiw's best, so he plowed into the common Tier version.

Once he got past the grotesque twists, and the opaque phras-
ing, he became fascinated. The way humans chose to impart
information, especially engineering information, revealed so
much about them, he wondered why this wasn't standard
course material for all Ardr.

Gradually he became aware of a semirhythmic thudding
against the wall. When the intensity increased, he suddenly
knew what he was hearing. Despite himself, he listened and
compared, wondering what it implied about the human nervous system. He'd always assumed that if they were going to
do it in a cabin, they'd do it in the shower since cabins didn't
have ponds. But obviously they were using the bed. Then he
remembered the huge group in the water with the spectators
cheering them on. Humans were certainly diversified.

He sank back to his reading. It would be a very long time until any female chose him again, so it was best not to think about it. At all.

On the other hand, he was even more convinced that the key to understanding the human threat to Ardr lay in the peculiarities of human sexuality—or at least in the bonds their practices ritualized.

About half an hour later, voices roused him from the intricacies of evacuation protocols.

" . . . heard about it! Walt, it's all over the ship."

"I don't want . . . against Grummon! Indiw . . ."

"Indiw again! Damn that . . ."

"Marla, you're . . . Indiw . . . promotion . . . career!"

"Pit Bull Two should be my . . . your choice!"

" . . . Indiw's as long as . . ."

" . . . Pit Bull Three then!"

" . . . wingman? . . . pair."

" . . . move up when Indiw . . ."

"Marla!" It was a roar that fairly shook the wall and stopped her barely audible tirade. " . . . not in Pit Bull!"

"Indiw again! . . ."

Chancy had coveted the slot that Indiw now held as Falstaff's wingman, and now that Falstaff had been promoted and given the right to choose the new members for the squadron, Chancy naturally assumed he'd choose her. But obviously he hadn't. And she blamed Indiw.

" . . . rid of him!"

"He'll . . . own good time!"

There was an anguished squall, and the front of the cabin vibrated so hard Indiw thought something had exploded. But it was only Falstaff's cabin door being abused.

Indiw wondered if humans became more irritable *after* sex. It would be an odd evolutionary quirk, if true.

With supreme discipline he went back to reading, cradling

a glass of the interesting drink in one hand and the slate in the other. And he began to make good progress.

Some hours later, when he was three quarters of the way through the last nodule, Daily Procedures, there was a loud noise.

He jumped, half expecting the predicted drill to have arrived, but the sound repeated. It was really a soft, chiming tone, hardly an alarm. And the monitor screen was flashing.

He fumbled at the controls, working through the instructions he'd just read. Falstaff appeared. There was something odd about his smile.

"Hey, ol' buddy. I hate to drink alone. Could use some company. You got any of that bottle left?"

"About nine tenths of it."

"Didn't like it?"

"Love it. I'm almost finished with the reading you recommended."

"Bring your bottle over here, and we can discuss ship's rules over a friendly drink. Come on, what do you say?"

There was just enough of the potent liquor in his system that Indiw seriously considered trying it. "Surely you could find another companion." Why had Falstaff forgotten Ardr don't socialize as humans do?

The human eyes looked squarely out of the screen, and with strangely soft movements of his head, Falstaff said, "Fresh out of companions. Nobody else on this bucket has been through what you and I have—together. Come on, one little drink won't hurt you. Honest, I don't bite—or claw—my drinking buddies."

Drinking buddies. It was a status of intimacy fabricated from alien concepts welded haphazardly together. But it held a mysterious fascination. After all he'd lost today, who was there to condemn him for this perversion? He'd been onto Falstaff's ground so often already that he was fairly sure he wouldn't go berserk and rip the human's guts out in a territorial reflex. Falstaff's quarters didn't smell any different from the public areas of the ship. But of course now they'd reek of Chancy, too. And other activities.

But nobody would see them. The Ardr pilots surely wouldn't leave the "habitat" the humans had built for them. They'd be comfortably asleep by now—having nightmares about him. Especially Rkizzhi.

"Come on, Indiw. What're friends for if not to get through the long, difficult nights."

"I'm coming." Before he could change his mind, he snapped the nodule case shut and stowed it, grabbed the bottle and his glass, then went next door. He'd been right. Falstaff's place reeked of Chancy—and fulminating scents that had to be human sex, oddly meaningless scents that stirred nothing in him.

The human wore a shapeless exercise suit. His feet were bare. They were ugly and impotent feet, with one oddly shaped toe that looked as if it had been broken and not set properly. Clearly this was why humans wore boots.

Falstaff had folded the bed up into a couch, a trick Indiw had found in one of the manuals he'd read. It certainly increased the floor area. Seated at one end, Falstaff had his half-empty bottle, a glass, and a case of colorful nodules beside him, various issues of some kind of entertainment publication with pictures.

"Welcome, welcome, dearest friend, to whom I owe my life many times over—after less than four days association. Little did I know when I first laid eyes on you that you'd save my life and make my fortune! Salut!" He tipped his glass and gulped.

Indiw averted his gaze and busied himself by settling onto the other end of the folded bed, filling his glass.

While Indiw fussed, Falstaff continued, "Little did I know that you'd put me into the history books! Salut!" He drank again. "Little did I know that you'd pay such a price to avert a scandal I'd never hear the end of. Salut!"

Intellectually, he understood Falstaff was paying him honor. He tried to keep his claws retracted. "Please. Stop. Don't."

Waving his half-full glass in the air, Falstaff said, "I have to propose one more toast. I can't drink to you without drinking to Freddy Desplaine, wherever he is!" His unsteady hand swooped the sloshing glass toward his mouth and Indiw looked away, nearly dropping his own glass.

"Come on, come on, you have to drink to a toast, especially the first toast to a departed soul."

"Departed soul?"

"Freddy was my wingman. Bought it defending *Katukin*. How could you not drink to that?"

How indeed? It wasn't his way of honoring the dead, but then shouldn't one honor the dead in the way the dead would understand?

Closing his eyes, he raised his glass in the gesture Falstaff had used and repeated, "To Freddy Desplaine, wherever he is!" He brought the glass to his mouth, told his stomach firmly that Falstaff was not even there, and managed to touch his tongue to the liquid. It had an aroma that blocked out most of the stray human effluvia.

There was a long, long silence, and finally Indiw dared to look. Falstaff's glass was empty and he was staring into the bottom of it with a peculiarly tense expression.

Indiw reached over and poured some liquid into the glass. "Freddy must have been 'one helluva pilot.' "

"Yeah, he was that. But how did you know?"

"He flew with you. Can't imagine anyone but the best keeping up with you."

The human's grin was only a forlorn attempt at a response. Then he dropped it, and swung his glass again. "To Freddy Desplaine, best g'ddamn pilot in the Fleet!"

This time Falstaff's glass touched Indiw's with a ping. Falstaff stopped, watching him. "Well?" he prompted.

Indiw echoed the toast. This time it was easier to complete the ceremony.

Falstaff swallowed, and, lips drawn in a straight line, said, "To Freddy, best g'ddamn friend a man could have." Then he tossed back the rest of the liquid without raising his glass.

Indiw watched, horrified fascination warring with the abrupt realization that something had changed for Falstaff. A moment later the human was doubled over, knees drawn up, one arm propped over them and face buried in the crook of the bent elbow. His body was convulsing, bouncing the couch as sounds tore out of his throat, unmodulated groans of agony.

Indiw swore. "I'll call the medics!" he said quietly and scrambled to his feet going for the monitor.

"No!" gasped Falstaff.

Indiw checked. "But—"

Falstaff made a more familiar sound, and finally Indiw understood. The human was crying. It was grief for his wingman.

Silently Indiw faded back toward the door, abandoning his bottle, intent only on restoring the man's privacy. Humans considered it disgraceful to cry in public. But he found the door locked. As he fumbled with the mechanism, he realized that for Falstaff, that lock made this private space, even though there was someone else in it with him.

He turned to Falstaff who was still curled against the back of the bed, struggling with a catharsis very like the one that had seized Indiw upon discovering the intrusion into his quarters. It had to run its course properly if the man was to recover, and apparently he'd been invited to share this with Falstaff because his presence was necessary to the completion of the process.

Falstaff had allowed him his privacy; he would provide Falstaff his company.

He crept back to the bed, sitting on his end as lightly as an insect landing on a flower. He had no idea what might happen next, but he would get through it.

It took half of a standard Tier hour for Falstaff to subside. Once in a while, Indiw thought he heard "Marla" mixed in with the muttered "Freddy"'s. At last Falstaff rolled over to sit on the edge of the folded bed, head in his hands. He shook himself. "Oh, shit, I'm sorry. I don't know what came over me." He lunged to his feet, and wove unsteadily across the compartment to the facilities. The door shut behind him.

Indiw waited, sipping freely at his liquor with relief in the temporary, illusionary solitude, and thinking. He refilled his glass, and drank half of it down before he made himself stop. It was already affecting him. He hated what stuff like that did to his reflexes.

When Falstaff emerged, his hair was wet, his face blctchy. He leaned against the door cowling. "I—"

Indiw offered. "I should have left."

"No!" Falstaff stepped across the floor and sank down next to the couch, leaning his back against it, propping his elbows on his knees. "It took a lot for you to sit through that, didn't it?"

"You've made similar efforts on my behalf."

"Is that why? Gratitude?"

"I'm not sure I understand the concept *gratitude*. I chose to stay."

"Like you chose to stay with me out there. There must be reasons for choices, Indiw. Even Ardr have reasons."

"Sometimes not. Sometimes we only have motives."

"There's a difference?"

"Isn't there?"

"Do you mean Ardr instinct is motive, not reason?" Falstaff half turned to glance quickly up at Indiw. "You violated every instinct you own to stay here. Why?"

Why indeed? "Even if the expression may differ, I do understand grief. I understand loss. I understand that when a limb is amputated, the shock is not just physical. And that shock can be even worse when the amputated limb was not physical. It is a lesson—a very fresh lesson—I have learned."

Falstaff digested that for a long time. Then he reached for the half-full glass sitting on the floor beside him. He didn't seem to notice it was Indiw's glass. Watching Falstaff toss back the remainder of that liquid made Indiw cringe. He dug his claws into the bedding and refused to move.

After a while Falstaff said, "It must be heaven to fly with an Ardr wing that you really, really know, that moves to your own inner tempo, so you never even have to think about them, but just about what's attacking you." He rested his forehead on his hands, propping his arms on his knees. "It was like that with Freddy. One in a million. One in a lifetime. I thought. Until I flew with you."

He knows! Gods of the Universe, he knows! He felt the bedding parting under his claws. How could a human know? Deep inside him, a wall he'd so carefully built began to crumble. He could feel his own grief billowing out through the cracks. He didn't want it to happen. Not here.

"Indiw. Why did you report yourself as Pit Bull Four returning to *Tacoma?*"

"I thought—no, I felt—like Pit Bull Four. At least, I did while we were disposing of that Hyos. It seemed to need acknowledgment—that those who went, came back. So few did."

"A passing moment of insanity? I mean, what would the Third Wing pilots make of it?"

"What should they make of it?"

"Did they know you were getting the award?"

"Yes."

"Did they know you were going to turn it down?"

"Yes."

"What are they going to think when you turn up to fly back with them in the morning?"

"I don't really want to think about it." It might be his very last flight, ever. And it was going to be the hardest. The bodies on Rkizzhi's cargo transport. The distrust. The withdrawal. The hostility.

"It would have been okay if you'd managed to turn the award down, wouldn't it? Calling yourself Pit Bull Four. You could have passed it off as a joke or something."

"Or something."

"Indiw? I could get your temporary brevet to Pit Bull Two extended. Just until things blow over. You never applied for a transfer back to an Ardr ship, so you don't have to go back with them tomorrow."

"That would make things worse."

"How could it be worse? You said that the award would destroy your life. That you'd never be accepted."

"Well. Maybe. Or maybe I can change that."

"Maybe if you wait awhile, you'd have a better chance. Here, that award could make your career."

He wants me to stay and fly with him! Indiw had never considered that idea. "Why would you want me to stay? As long as I'm here, Marla Chancy isn't going to be content. And in my experience, there's nothing worse than a female who isn't content." *Oh, why did I say that?*

Falstaff twisted to look up at him again. Then he looked hard at the wall next to the bed. "Oh, Lord, you heard all that?"

Horns aching with embarrassment, Indiw asked, "All what? Did I miss something?"

Falstaff threw his head back and laughed, a wild free sound of delight. "Oh, Indiw, you are the best! Won't you just consider staying—for a while?"

"I don't understand why you'd want that."

"You saved my life, you *made* my career, and with three years pay to invest, I can retire when my time is up. I might even have two more promotions under my belt by then, and be able to retire in style."

"Is this an example of gratitude as motivation?"

Falstaff jerked his back away from the edge of the folded bed as if it had burned him. He turned, scowled, then settled back and said to the far wall. "Indiw, we've both known what a perfect flying partnership is like, and we've both found out what it means to lose that. Is it so easy to turn your back on a second chance at perfection? Or didn't it feel that good to you?"

Indiw remembered how they had circled that lone Hyos, not discussing how to handle it, but just falling into the cadenced pounding on its shields until it blazed out of existence. He remembered how he'd forgotten to cue Falstaff on an improvised weave, and found the human right behind him, anyway. "It felt that good."

"I knew it!" The human head fell back onto the propped arms. "If you want the spot, it's yours. I, for one, don't want to try flying with some klutz who's going to get me killed."

Indiw didn't think it a good idea to mention Chancy again. He didn't know why he hadn't seen this invitation coming. But now that it was staring at him, the choice seemed clear. He thought about it, turned it every which way, wondering at the bright, new excitement glowing in him. It was a way out. It had to be a way out. If he could survive dealing with Chancy.

"Falstaff." No answer. "Falstaff?"

The human's breathing was slow and heavy. *He's asleep.*

Indiw watched for a while, wondering if the human would wake. He thought about getting up to go. But that seemed like a gigantic effort. His whole body was just too heavy. He sloshed a bit more of the liquor into the glass beside Falstaff, and downed it in a few hefty swallows.

His last thought stretched and petered out slowly. *Drinking buddies. That's what it means. Drinking buddies.*

"Indiw? Indiw, wake up! Come on, guy, it's late, and Rkizzhi's been calling every five minutes searching for you."

With massive effort, Indiw unglued his eyes, then leapt to his feet, crouched for a fight to the death with the intruder. As his brain woke and retrieved his identity and pieced together his memory, his glands subsided and came under civilized control.

He swore behind his teeth, straightening and feeling every muscle complain. His brain felt swollen. His eyes fought his efforts to focus them.

Falstaff was standing well across the room, in the door of the facilities, granting him space. Then he heard what the man had said. Rkizzhi.

"If she calls again, tell her I'm on my way."

Looking both ways along the corridor, he let himself into his own place and stopped, coldly repelled by the ugly little compartment. He'd been insane—no, drunk—to entertain the notion of staying here. No amount of good flying was worth it.

By the time he arrived on the flight deck, his little bag packed, his head was clear and he was ready to face what must be faced. Or at least he'd thought he was ready.

As soon as he appeared, the Ardr who were dispersed along the line of waiting craft stopped what they were doing and watched him warily.

His fighter was at the very end of the line. He turned toward it, pretending to ignore the hostility. Would they choose not to travel with him? It was a long way to *Katular,* longer than on the way here. The ships were diverging, covering a huge territory between them.

He tossed his bag into the cockpit and climbed up, leaning

in to secure it in place. He was fumbling with the compartment's catch when Rkizzhi's voice wafted up to him. "Indiw! What did you do with that—*thing*—they gave you?"

She was standing by the ladder below him. He turned to look down at her. "Gave it back to them, unopened." That had been hard. He'd thought that the instructions for claiming the money would be in that case, too. But that money would do him more harm than good. So he'd left the case on the bed in his quarters still sealed.

"You made quite a spectacle standing with them."

She was the most hostile Ardr he'd ever faced. "I became convinced I'd be more of a spectacle if I were absent."

"Possibly." She turned to go, then paused and added, "You were right about one thing. This *has* been a unique experience. It's sated my appetite for a while." Then she climbed into the cargo transport.

Indiw slid into his own cockpit, sealed up, ran checks, and cleared with *Tacoma* launch control. But he hardly noticed what he was doing. His whole being was focused on the choice he was making. Only when his craft inserted into the launch alley did it occur to him that he should have spoken to Falstaff about his decision.

And then he was in space, streaking after the Ardr group, which was heading home at full throttle, breaking into battle maneuvers even as he chased them. Catching up kept him too busy to think, and that felt good. They let him catch up. But the message was plain. *We don't choose you.*

He didn't enter the maneuvering territory. He trailed them running a singleton pattern, and no one dropped back to weave him into the group. No one opened the weave to invite him in. No one even spoke to him.

They were beyond the edge of *Tacoma*'s flight control zone, beyond their instruments' awareness of the big carrier when the Hyos appeared.

CHAPTER SIX

THE HYOS HAD BEEN HEADING STRAIGHT FOR *TACOMA* before they encountered the Ardr flight. And there were a lot of them. This was completely different from the little skirmish Indiw had fought with Falstaff. Even his onboard computer couldn't count the Hyos fighters in this swarm. These were not survivors or scouts. This was a whole swarm on the move.

Indiw dropped back, turned, and raced to where his equipment could raise *Tacoma*. He snapped off the warning message. Not waiting for a reply, he returned to the combat, circling, looking for a way for one craft to make a difference before the Hyos spotted him. Already instrument readings were fuzzing out from all the stray energy erupting from the battle.

He saw what he thought might be an opening and went right for the middle of things, trying to cope with an unfamiliar weaving style and more Hyos than he could count.

One Ardr pilot shouted instructions to him. He took the advice, and in the space where he'd been two Hyos collided and flashed out of existence. He completed the weaving, took out another Hyos with his beam cannon, hit two more but didn't even slow them, and took a solid battering from three Hyos who seemed to have a grudge against him.

He escaped them into the thick of the battle weaving to the

outside just in time to see the cargo transport erupt into a ball of fire.

Rkizzhi! He got the one who did it, but in an odd way he was grateful to the Hyos. Now the last bodies of *Katukin*'s crew had been atomized as all the others of his wing had been, and he would soon be. Maybe. There was no more fitting way for him to die than reestablishing his right to claim land. Or if he couldn't regain the right to make his claim, he suddenly knew he didn't want to live to know about it.

He wove an improvisation through the space the cargo ship had occupied, tailed one Hyos and locked on manually while he nailed another down with his autotracker. He fired on both Hyos simultaneously. The power drain nearly extinguished his own shields. But he got both Hyos and, at the astonished reprimands from two Ardr, had to apologize for breaking pattern while his teeth rattled from another severe pounding they couldn't intercept because he was in the wrong place. He'd become accustomed to having Falstaff around.

"But Indiw's got the right idea," said someone else. "It's time for desperate measures before we run out of power."

Or fighters.

Those who were left, damaged, trailing sparkling rivulets of charged debris, broke into a freer stance, each with enough room to maneuver and fire on anything that came at them without danger of hitting one of their own.

The break maneuver confused the Hyos again, and Indiw got away from the one that had nearly penetrated his shields. He picked a target and went for it. Missed. Picked another and got it. The one he'd missed wallowed about comically wondering why he wasn't being chased—obviously accustomed to fighting humans.

Indiw screamed up the tail of another Hyos, scraping his energy shields against the Hyos's and pushing the Hyos into the streaking path of another Hyos. The explosion tossed

Indiw far from the impact point, his shields hardening against the radiation sleet, robbing his weapons of power.

When he regained control, he was on the edge of the swarm facing deep black space. And all there was behind him was a solid phalanx of Hyos fighters.

His computer confirmed it. No *Katular* transponders left. They only failed if a fighter was blown to dust. He upped the gain of his receiver. Nothing.

The swarm was forming up behind him, making a hollow pocket in which they expected to trap him. It was flattering, but he chose to decline the invitation to fight all of them at once.

As they moved up to englobe him, Indiw pulled out a tray of circuit boards. Barely glancing at what he was doing, he ripped out the safeties governing his energy usage. With his other hand, he cued up a program he'd devised but never thought he'd need.

At the exact moment when the Hyos formation had almost closed, he lined up on the closing aperture and engaged his program.

His shields disappeared, as if he were surrendering. Then, without any warning, his fighter shot out of the tiny hole at three times its top speed. He even managed to get off a volley of cannon shots as he passed. All the rest of his missiles were laid quietly, dark of all energy usage, in his wake.

A split second later, bright fire blossomed all across the Hyos swarm's near edge, effectively screening Indiw's retreat from their instruments. He would never know how many fighters he'd taken out that time.

Then the g's piled up, immobilizing him. He would die. But they would never know it. The surviving Hyos would be even more wary of Ardr from now on.

He blacked out. He wasn't sure for how long. When he came to the gravity was slacking off. The program had disengaged when the instruments no longer registered Hyos.

Gradually his fighter's functions were returning to normal, complete with shields and internal gravity. A quick check after he reengaged the safeties revealed that neither his person nor his fighter's circuitry had taken serious radiation damage, though concussion damage was eating into most machine functions. And he still had fuel. Even as he watched, his shields came back to full power with only one weak spot where he'd taken a pounding. Sweet program. And to think he'd only tested it on simulator.

When his forward view focused, he found that right in front of him—right exactly in front of him—was the neat array of a human fighter wing's formation, coming head on and accelerating.

"Pit Bull Two, is that you out there? Are you alive?"

Still dizzy and stunned, he answered, "No, this is Indiw. Used to be Pit Bull Four."

Falstaff's voice whooped, "Two, you idiot. Two! You're Pit Bull Two—at least until this afternoon. Fall in, wingman, we've some Hyos ass to kick."

"A whole lot more than you think." He gave a quick reprise of the battle. As he spoke, his display flashed and converted to the human tactical signal Falstaff was sending him. He found Falstaff flying alone at one side of the formation. According to what he'd read last night, that was strictly against regulations.

He had to move out of the formation's way or disrupt their pattern, so he moved toward Falstaff, who demanded, "Damage report, Pit Bull Two."

Indiw reeled off the list of malfunctions and confessed to being on backup systems here and there.

Another voice, deep, gravelly, preempted Falstaff. "Good work, Pit Bull Two. But you're out of it now. Falstaff, take him home."

"B-b- . . . Captain Hansen—"

"That's an order, Falstaff. We've acquired target."

"Yes, sir." Falstaff didn't sound happy.

Commentary broke out, profane with awe for the sheer numbers of Hyos ships out there. Indiw heard some memorable tributes to the Ardr flyers. A handful of Ardr had held that swarm long enough for the wing to scramble and meet them far enough from *Tacoma* to give them room to fight.

Falstaff peeled off and began a long, lazy circle back in consideration of Indiw's uncertain condition. "Come on, Indiw, you need a repair dock."

"You're not just going to leave, are you?"

"They only let me come because you were stuck out here with all that. You're my wingman."

The distance between them was opening as Falstaff set course for *Tacoma* and Indiw eased out into a weaving that would take him back to the battle.

Falstaff reversed and came up on Indiw's tail. "Indiw, what the hell's the matter with you? I thought we had this all straightened out last night, and then you just take off without a word—and now—Indiw, we've got our orders!"

"I don't take orders. I have a battle to finish."

"Indiw, *Tacoma*'s going to need protection. There's another whole swarm of Hyos coming from the opposite direction. The Admiral brought us reinforcements and supplies from Aberdeen, but we're still undermanned. We've got to get you in for repairs so we can fly with the next wing to go out. Come on, guy."

"Do what you choose. I have a battle to finish." He drove up along the outside of the formation, picked up the leading edge of the Hyos, groped into the back of his mind to remember how to calculate the movements of human formations, chose a target, and broke out of the pack streaking for the enemy.

"*Pit* Bull!" yelled the deep voice.

Only then did Indiw notice that Falstaff was right beside him. But it was too late. He entered the Hyos swarm firing dead ahead, blew two of them to fireballs and drove right through the glowing debris into the heart of the swarm.

After all the loss inflicted by the small contingent of Ardr, it was still a gigantic swarm, bigger than anything he'd ever fought. This swarm had to have at its protected center a Breeder's ship as well as their vital cargo ships with colonizing equipment.

But, oddly enough, they weren't on direct course for Aberdeen or any other nearby planet, though they might be evading *Katular*'s defense of Sinaha, maneuvering into Sinaha from an unexpected direction. But that was so unlike Hyos! He shoved it all aside. There was no time to think. Now, he was too busy.

Falstaff took on two Hyos to Indiw's right, and Indiw dove through the hole he made and widened it by two more fighters. Falstaff went under him, firing missiles, swooped ahead, and came above the reference plane with canons slamming at another Hyos that stood and battered him back. Indiw got in a lucky shot at the Hyos and it turned into a throbbing ball of light.

Indiw went through the hole, kept it from closing on Falstaff by heading straight for one Hyos until it was forced to move out of his path, and then fired his cannon at the ship behind that one.

Falstaff circled to Indiw's left, dropped a missile, and took the point once more. Scrambling to avoid Falstaff's missile, two Hyos collided. One bounced, shields solid, and the other exploded. Indiw streaked through the hole, boring into the thick of the swarm. Falstaff followed, protecting Indiw's weak shield, soaking up solid hits, hardly saying a word other than muttered curses.

They did it again and again until it was a wonder the Hyos

hadn't caught on to their method. But the Hyos had an entire human wing to contend with.

And the humans *were* making headway. The density of Hyos around Indiw was definitely thinning.

Indiw worried about his fuel and power. The board was redlining all the weapons systems, but he'd seen how far one of these fighters could go on red. If he could just get to the Breeder ship, he could ram it if he had nothing else left to get it with.

Falstaff circled him again, led the way through the next wall of Hyos, dropped down as Indiw pounded through the hole he'd made, circled back as Indiw picked off Falstaff's pursuers, and led the way at the next wall of Hyos, emitting missiles in a wide burst. Indiw followed him through the wall of Hyos, and then they were at the center of the swarm.

But there was nothing there. Nothing except Hyos fighters—the little single-seaters they'd been fighting—and two huge tanker ships carrying their spare fuel.

"It's not here," said Falstaff. "I could have sworn they were protecting a Breeder!"

Indiw hadn't said a word about any Breeder ship. Falstaff just thought the same way he did. "Well, let's take the tankers. They can't get to any Tier planet without them."

"Right."

It was a hard fight. Suddenly all the Hyos in the vicinity considered the two lone fighters a serious threat. Indiw took another solid hit, and sparks flew in the cockpit. His helmet and visor kept him from being burned, but his flight suit was scored. It might not hold up to vacuum.

Falstaff used his last missile on one of the tankers and missed. But then the other tanker, maneuvering to avoid the expected debris of the first one, was hit by the missile, which couldn't tell the difference between the two identical ships.

The explosion ripped holes in Indiw's outer shields, and

his particle alarms shrilled. When the particle storm cleared, another group of control circuits had been fried.

He worked frantically to regain directional control. Falstaff, separated from him by a scattering of Hyos, stood off three fighters with a dance of loops and turns that would have done an Ardr stunt pilot proud.

Suddenly four humans, a tightly formed squadron, broke through that final wall of Hyos. With their leader snapping orders, two joined Falstaff and two circled Indiw. Another Hyos cannon hit Indiw, on his weak side, and he figured he didn't have much time left.

Hiding behind his human defenders, he patched all his remaining weapons power into his one functional cannon and locked on to the surviving tanker. On the other side of the tanker, just at the edge of Indiw's instrument range, Falstaff and his two compatriots pounded away at the tanker's shields whenever they could slip clear of their attackers.

Watching Falstaff, Indiw timed his last shot, and loosed it.

He was surprised when his own ship didn't blow up from the overloads he'd built. He was utterly astonished when the tanker sprouted a trail of white mist, ignited, and slowly turned into a rolling gout of green flame that waxed white-hot and then invisible. But even more incredibly, the Hyos departed, all at once, fleeing. Wave after wave of them hit lightspeed and disappeared.

Indiw's remaining instruments screamed warnings of the particle blitz from their wake and the exploding tanker, and his shields hardened—feebly.

He looked around with what was left of his instruments, and there were dozens of human transponders still active out there. Dozens and dozens.

But he assumed their instruments were screaming warnings also, which was why they didn't try to deploy a supralight net and pull the escaping Hyos back down to battle speed.

Before Indiw had caught his breath, the now familiar gravelly voice said, "What is it with you, Falstaff? This hero business going to your head or something?"

"No, sir. Communications problem."

"You heard me just fine!"

"Yes, sir. But my partner couldn't understand me. Thought I said to charge them. Sorry, sir. Won't happen again."

The silence from the other humans as they formed up around their wing commander was total, but it lasted only a moment.

Indiw could see the holes in the human formation, the tattered lace the Hyos had made of an entire fighter wing. Snapping off damage reports and calling muster, they reorganized their formation and limped back toward *Tacoma,* going at the rate the slowest among them could make.

Halfway there, the leader ordered a small group to detach and go to full throttle. Several of the pilots were bleeding and couldn't manage to stay conscious long enough to get home unless they cast off and went at maximum speed.

Indiw wasn't feeling too wonderful himself, but said nothing. They'd repair his ship and he could take more Hyos with him when he died. Or maybe his flight recorders would be enough to redeem him from disgrace. He knew he'd fought well, even if he had spent a lot of time and ammunition on Hyos who were after Falstaff. The two of them had gotten the Hyos tankers, leaving those fighters stranded.

But where had they run to? He puzzled over that for a long while, realizing that his brain wasn't up to speed.

Finally he noticed his board. The ragged and blurred displays were mostly useless, and he'd been discounting their information for some time now. But the fuel indicator had turned an odd shade of deep red he'd never seen before. And now his thrusters had quit.

"Pit Bull One, I've got a problem. I've lost maneuvering

power. No fuel. And I'm headed directly at *Tacoma*."

"Shit. How long ago did this happen?"

"I just noticed."

"Are you all right, Indiw? I can barely hear you."

"I'm all right."

"Indiw? Can you hear me?" Falstaff's voice was faint. It was impossible to tell exactly where he was, but he couldn't be that far away.

Indiw tried everything he could think of to restore the signal, but as he worked, his lighting failed. Gravity had gone a while back, he wasn't sure when. All these systems were separately powered and separately backed up, but when he'd pulled the safeties, he'd combined and drained all the stored backup power for the different systems. He'd been able to keep going as his thrusters supplied power, but now everything was gone. Only his tactical display was limping along, flashing and shaking and smearing.

Very faintly, amid a hissing roar of static, Falstaff's voice said, "Pit Bull Two, stand by. Captain Hansen, Pit Bull has a problem."

In a kind of bemused fog, Indiw listened to the fading signal as the humans handled the problem "through channels."

The battered wing broke and reconfigured, strung out in a long line, some going ahead of Indiw, others who were in better shape hanging back as rear guard.

When they reached *Tacoma,* the landing bays all had their doors open, and flashing warning signals outlined every dish projector protruding from the skin of the ship.

The carrier had deployed all its formidable weapons array. Even the big main projector that could boil a hole in the mantle of a planet almost to the core was exposed and limned in bright orange in hopes that none of the returning fighters would crash into it and disarm the big ship.

As Indiw squinted helplessly at his failing displays, *Tacoma* maneuvered to align one landing bay outlined in red haze with Indiw's inert trajectory.

Tacoma's crash fields bloomed to full strength. None of Indiw's landing gear would deploy, not even his own emergency crash fields. It was all dead. He just rode it in. There was not one single thing he could do.

And then everything went black.

"Indiw? Indiw! Come oh, Indiw, don't make a liar out of me. You can do it. Come on, man!"

It was Falstaff's voice, far away but urgent. The air reeked pungently. It was a vaguely familiar odor. And there were sounds, little blurpy pings and dings dancing musically about— human designed instruments talking to their masters in sound instead of smell.

"You'd better go now. He might not come out of it until tomorrow."

"Indiw! Say something. Anything. Come on, curse me out for a fool or something."

"Walt," whispered Indiw. His mouth didn't form the whole word. He noticed how his face hurt, his body ached, and taking inventory, he realized he was thirsty.

He opened his eyes. "Walt." The pale face swam into focus. "What are you doing here? Where are we?"

As he worked the muscles, his mouth became more cooperative. And his eyes focused. He was in the humans' hospital. No wonder he felt so bad. There was no tree, no sap, nothing. "And how's my fighter?"

"Totaled. Mine, too. But don't worry. The engineers will have rebuilt ones for us soon."

Someone in white crowded into his personal space, then bent over him detaching leads and silencing machinery, saying in a soft voice, "You're going to be fine. You weren't hurt too badly, and the supplies you brought with you from *Katular* let us fix you up. The radiation was the worst, but all that danger's past now. You've suffered no reproductive harm at all, though you've collected some nice bruises in rather unfortunate places."

"You mean I'm not going to die?"

"Not a chance. Do you really feel that bad?"

"I don't know. I never died before."

Human laughter, Falstaff joining in with a relieved note. "Indiw, you are something!"

Filled with reassurances, Falstaff left. After drinking a huge amount of vile-tasting water, Indiw was able to nibble at the ration packs they brought for him. They even left him alone so he could eat. But he fell asleep in midbite, not even noticing how the bedding material irritated his hide.

When he woke, the room was dim and there was no one about. He got up, and racking his memory for details he thought he'd never need again, he found his way to his own place, hoping it hadn't been assigned to anyone else yet.

It hadn't. In fact, the little sliding plaque next to the door now displayed his name. His travel case sat outside the door with a new flight suit and another uniform in a carrier beside it. Inside, his award case was still on the bed as he'd left it, and there were no foreign scents around. He pushed the award onto the floor, tossed his travel case and the clothing on top of it, and flopped onto the soft platform, falling back into the depths of exhaustion.

When he woke again, all hell was breaking loose around him. Lights flashed, there were blatts and shrieks, a noise like he'd never heard, and then the deck shuddered.

Before he knew what he was doing, he was on his feet tripping over the items he'd left scattered, searching out his goggles, scrambling into the new flight suit and boots. Anything that could shake a carrier like that was serious. Very serious.

When he opened his door, he was greeted with billowing smoke, the clatter of running humans in boots, Captain Sutcliff calmly enunciating orders over the emergency speakers, alarms whooping, and through the smoke, panels with written instructions flashing in various colors. Falstaff was right. The light changed for emergencies—drill or no.

Indiw watched the chaos develop, stricken with amazement that such a species had risen to space travel. The more dire the emergency, the more orders they needed.

But despite the voice of the ship's captain, the chaos increased. With each explosion or clattering-clang, their movements became ever more randomized. More and more, they questioned each other about what to do. Nothing Indiw had read had prepared him for the actuality of humans responding to an emergency.

"Indiw! This way!"

It was Falstaff's voice but he couldn't see him through the smoke.

A hand grabbed his elbow and yanked. He went with it, stumbling. They came to a point where someone was handing out breathing filters to each person who passed. Indiw took one and strapped it on. At least that was a piece of equipment Ardr and humans could share, if necessary. His nose, already seared from the smoke, didn't care that the filter also took all other olfactory clues with it.

Then he ran behind Falstaff and some others. They seemed to know where they were going and what they were doing. Maybe the chaos wasn't really chaos at all. Maybe he just didn't understand that the situation was under control.

Passing another human stationed by a bulkhead locker, Indiw felt a long weapon smack into his chest. Automatically his hands closed over it, claws extending to cradle the stock securely. At least it was familiar, a standard Tier issue beamer. Fully charged. It just lacked padding for his claws, but he'd drilled with unpadded weapons many times.

Falstaff shouted in his ear, "This way! Hurry!"

They came to a T intersection and turned up the side corridor. And then they were prone behind a barricade of cargo containers, Falstaff on his right. The beamer's scope penetrated the smoke and Indiw saw ranks of squat forms—with beamers—shooting—at him.

He shot back before his conscious mind had identified the outlines as Hyos. They were quite distinctive. Oblong, bulbous heads mounted on short necks, a disproportionately squat torso, and long, long, long spindly legs that bent every which way. Their two wiry arms also had multiple jointing. They were quite graceful.

He hit one squarely in the midsection, their most vulnerable spot, but it kept coming. "Body armor!" he yelled over the noise. Some of that noise had to be air whistling out of *Tacoma* into space. "Aim for the head!"

He tried again, missed, and on his third shot downed one of the attackers.

A human in a flight suit slammed down at his left elbow, prone, jammed a beamer snout through a crack in the barricade, and steadily squeezed off a shot. It skewered a Hyos who fell in the path of two others and caused the whole mob of them to slow down. The human's breather-masked face turned toward him. "You're Indiw, aren't you?"

Even muffled, he knew the voice. "Commander Chancy! Yes, I'm Indiw." His next shot splashed off a Hyos helmet. He took a deep breath, his toe claws digging hard into the soles of his flight boots, and squeezed off a careful shot. His target dropped.

"Nice shot," she muttered.

"Aim for the lower central quadrant of the face! Only vulnerable spot I've found so far."

"Got one!" grunted Falstaff.

The others on that firing line took Indiw's advice and began downing targets producing a low fence of bodies marking their farthest effective range. Indiw wondered what was happening on the rest of the ship. Was this the only incursion?

To the humans, the words EMERGENCY ALERT written in red everywhere seemed to satisfy their curiosity. But he needed more. He needed to know what was going on so he could choose where he could be most effective.

"Get your head down, Pilot!" barked Captain Hansen's voice behind him.

Indiw realized he'd been raising up to look around. He took the man's suggestion. Someone behind him fired something large and noisy. A missile whizzed through the spot where his head had been. Out in front, a whump-pop erupted, and the corridor filled with splattered purple blood. Hyos blood.

Through the slippery swamp and over the pile of bodies another wave of Hyos surged toward them, the lead rank firing in unison. Chancy and Falstaff fired in cadence, creating two holes to either side of the middle of that charging line. Indiw connected them by removing the eight Hyos in the middle. More from behind filled in the gap.

Someone to the far left grunted and sighed out his life. Hansen growled, "Chancy, come here!"

Chancy and Falstaff twisted to look behind them while Indiw kept firing. Then Falstaff yelled, "Hansen, no! Get someone else! You don't need a marksman to fire that thing!"

Chancy hissed, "Stay out of this, Falstaff!"

"Hell I will! He needs volunteers for suicide, and I'm not letting you volunteer."

Absently picking and dropping targets, Indiw struggled to reconcile the concept *volunteer* with the concept *permission*. Fighting beside the humans, it seemed crucial to understand because *volunteer* was one of the rough glosses for *choose,* and he'd had a lot of trouble communicating that lately. He kept firing steadily without making a dent in the supply of Hyos assault troops. They were ground-trained assault troops, the kind a landholder would have to face if the space defense failed.

Falstaff and Chancy were still faced off in a glaring match when another reeking human body wriggled up on Indiw's left. It was a woman, bleeding heavily from the stump of her right leg, which was roughly pressure bandaged. There was another bandage around her ribs. "Move it, Chancy. This one's my shot."

Chancy rolled aside to make room for the woman, studied her, then gave a single jerky nod. Then she turned back to the Hyos. So did Falstaff, and suddenly there was a gap in the Hyos line again. The ends of that approaching line were also wilting where other humans at the barricade were concentrating their fire.

As Indiw worked, he was conscious of Hansen and the others behind him frantically opening cases and slapping weapons parts together. A man wormed up to the wounded woman, seated a cradle device on the woman's shoulder, and backed off while she squirmed comfortable under the rigging, checking it out with the economic touches of an expert.

"Okay," she called without turning. Then a very large tube edged up on Indiw's left. He missed·a shot as it nudged his arm.

"Sorry," shouted someone in his ear.

He dropped the next target while two men lifted the weapon barrel onto the woman's shoulder rig.

She yelled, "Hit the deck!"

When Indiw neglected to accept the suggestion, preferring to try a long shot to nail one of the Hyos directing operations from the rear, Falstaff flung one arm over Indiw's shoulders and, despite the instant Ardr reflex response, dragged Indiw down behind the barricade.

Falstaff ended up half sprawled on top of Indiw, hands clamped over Indiw's wrists to prevent him from using his claws. "Easy, guy, easy," he crooned into Indiw's ear. A rising hum broke into a scream and exploded. Everything went red.

"Who told you to use that in here!" roared an outraged human at the end of the line. Indiw sympathized. He hadn't thought they'd load that thing with ground-rated shells.

"Captain Sutcliff's orders," shouted Captain Hansen. "They've gassed the alter-day crew's quarters. We're going to lose the ship to them if we can't stop them here."

"Shit!"

"Down!" shouted the wounded woman and loosed another blood-spattering round and everything went orange. Indiw could feel the heat right through the seven-crate-deep barricade. And those were space-shipping crates!

As Indiw's claws retracted, Falstaff let go of Indiw's wrists. "All right?"

"Sorry. You saved my life." If he'd been on top of the barricade when that round went off, he'd be scorched to a cinder. As he dragged his weapon back up to firing position, he saw through the seared purple gore that even the bulkheads were deformed from the heat blast.

Indiw squeezed off several more shots, got another Hyos, but the corridor was quickly jammed with them again. Two humans wriggled up behind the wounded female with a reload. He hadn't seen clearly what they'd been loading the thing with, but he thought this round looked to be a different color. But who could tell in this light?

Then the wounded female was ready with the heat weapon again, the grin on her face needing no translation. It was definitely a woman's weapon, that thing. He renewed his resolve never again to make an enemy of a human female.

"All right, guys," she called, "this is it. Take cover!"

This time, when Falstaff gripped his shoulder, Indiw chose to follow him back down the barricade through the thickening smoke and around the corner in the main corridor. Surely even the humans couldn't see a thing.

"Sound off!" yelled Hansen over the din of the Hyos weapons coming at them fast.

Each human yelled one number while Falstaff yelled two. Hansen called, "Let 'er rip!" Indiw thought the Captain's voice came from up by the barricade.

The next moment the world turned green.

"Shit, they got her!" whispered Falstaff.

When the green abated, Indiw saw the bulkhead opposite the side corridor had blackened. A quick glance around the corner revealed a scene of mass destruction. The barricade was melted to slag. The two humans who'd stayed behind it to lay down covering fire for the retreat were nothing but bones and outlines scorched into the deck. The remains of the huge weapon were sinking through the melting barricade. There was no trace of the wounded woman's body. The heat was intolerable.

That had obviously not been exactly what Hansen had planned to have happen. The Hyos were still coming.

There were five people gathered behind Falstaff. Captain Hansen wasn't one of them. Falstaff glanced around, straightened his shoulders, and commanded, "All right, fall back. Let's see if we can get word to the bridge. Follow me."

Even as they ran after Falstaff, Indiw heard Hyos scuffling over the barricade. Even Hyos would want to get through that heated section fast. Indiw remembered something from his reading—had it only been last night? "Walt, the service port!"

"Right." Even as Indiw spoke, Falstaff had stopped at one of the inconspicuous maintenance hatches. He had it open and they were inside as fast as they could scramble. When it shut behind them, total darkness engulfed them.

Indiw pulled his goggles and his breathing filter down to hang around his neck. The air was clearer. And no, it wasn't dark. There was a dim reddish glow.

Someone asked, "Can Hyos see by emergency lighting?"

"Doubt it," said Chancy. "But let's not risk it. Here." She opened a locker and handed out tools and lengths of pipe.

Very, very quietly, without any direction or consultation, the humans used the tools to attach loops to the hatch and immobilize it using the pipe. If the Hyos had studied manuals of the ship, they still wouldn't be able to open the hatch, and wouldn't know why until they'd gained access to the maintenance system some other way.

Meanwhile, Falstaff had moved off into the gloom. Indiw tracked him by smell. The human odor easily penetrated his smoke-irritated nose. Falstaff had found a com station. He looked over his shoulder at Indiw as he worked at the controls. "It's dead."

"Let me see." Indiw removed the protective panel and squinted at the wiring. It was all Tier standard, which could easily be their undoing if the Hyos had done their research well. "Here," said Indiw, disconnecting a board and improvising a jumper. "Try it now."

"Sutcliff here!"

"Pilot Commander Falstaff. B-deck, Corridor C intersection. The Hyos are through and heading for the bridge. I've got six survivors in the starboard maintenance shaft. Two slightly wounded. Three weapons. Orders, sir?"

He was answered by static. Indiw jiggled the circuit boards but it did no good. "Signal's gone. Now what do you do? How do you tell who's supposed to give the orders?"

"It's called chain of command. The senior officer left alive gives the orders, and if you're the last one left, you give yourself orders. Right now, it's my call."

Now that he mentioned it, Indiw remembered about "chain of command." He'd seen it during battle, and then again just now when Captain Hansen was killed. Falstaff must have read the insignia on everyone else's uniforms and figured out that he was to give orders. Then he just made the choices for everyone, and they just accepted it. What had been intellectual knowledge before suddenly became very real to Indiw. "All right. I choose to do what you decide."

Shaking his head in an odd rhythm, Falstaff led the way back to squat down by the others. He could probably see a little better than Indiw could, but Indiw could smell them.

"I think we may have lost the bridge," opened Falstaff in a low whisper. "We're certainly out of communication and on our own. We can't do anything against this size boarding party, so we've got to retreat, secure our own survival, find out what's going on, then maybe join up with other survivors and get word out—probably to *Katular* if we can't reach Aberdeen. Then we kick Hyos ass—right off this ship."

"Tall order," said Chancy, the only female among them.

"Think we can handle it?" asked Falstaff.

"You bet," she said.

A man said, "The Hyos just got our attention. That was unwise of them."

"Knew I could count on you." Falstaff's grin had a strange—almost feminine—quality. Indiw suppressed a shiver and decided maybe, when sufficiently irritated, human males might be just as formidable as their females. "Well, where shall we set up our headquarters? Suggestions?"

Another man, slender with bright blond hair, offered, "Aft of here, we set up the habitat for the Ardr. It's still there, I think. We partitioned off a section of a cargo hold, and there's a space behind the partition that's not on any map of the ship. The partition was made air and soundproof because the Ardr are so damn sensitive to odor and sound," he broke off and nodded at Indiw, "no offense, sir—and I can't imagine a prize crew taking time to do housekeeping chores down in that empty hold. They'll never notice that partition."

"You in maintenance, mister?" asked Falstaff.

"Lieutenant Osgood, sir, Purser's Office."

"You shoot damn good for a purser."

"Thank you, sir!"

"Anybody got a better idea?" Silence. "Know the way to this haven, Osgood?"

"Yes, sir. Follow me."

They trooped through the gloom single file. The most ominous thing was the sudden lack of sound. Even the vibrations and shakings had ceased. The alarms died out. And just as they arrived at another hatch, the regular lights came on. The Hyos knew how to operate at least some parts of a Tier ship.

The space the purser had found for them was large, adequately ventilated, cooler than the rest of the stuffy human ship, private, and dark. Someone brought in some portable lights and strung them up. A huge stack of crates was secured against the bulkhead at one end of the space. The rest was clean and bare.

"Home," announced Falstaff. He turned to survey those standing behind him. Pointing with one finger, he assigned jobs. "Make this place livable. Get us rations and medical supplies—and don't forget Indiw. Secure our perimeter. See about weapons. Osgood, you and Indiw hack into *Tacoma*'s main brain and work out a way to spy on these bastards. I'm going to reconnoiter for survivors. Three hours. Back here to report. Go!"

CHAPTER
SEVEN

★

IT WAS ALMOST SEVEN HOURS LATER THAT INDIW, SENIOR
to Osgood in rank, stood to report their findings in front of
several dozen battle-worn humans seated cross-legged on the
bare deck of their hiding place, facing him with rapt attention.
Falstaff and Chancy sat touching hip to hip at the back of the
crowd.

The air was redolent of unwashed human and pungent with
human food rations, which the humans ate at any odd moment
regardless of who was watching. Medical people were moving
wounded into the area behind the listeners while Indiw dug his
toe claws into his boots, blocking it all out and concentrating
just on what he had to say.

Having described what the clever Osgood had done to get
into the *Tacoma* system files, which the Hyos had altered to
their purposes, Indiw recounted how they had tapped into the
ship's intercom system turning it into a spy device.

"We found out what the Hyos are up to, but we were unable
to access *Tacoma*'s external communications. We're not even
sure if the ship still has any external com capacity. There's no
way to warn anyone of what's happened, unless we could get
a message capsule off. But they'd surely spot that and destroy
it." Indiw looked away from someone who was eating, struggling not to react.

"And exactly what are the Hyos up to?" prompted someone.

Indiw took a deep breath and willed himself to continue. "We're dealing with a coalition of three swarms making a concerted effort to punch a hole in the Tier defensive line and settle both Aberdeen and Sinaha at once. Swarms *never* ally like this. Never."

Falstaff swore, and some of the others made inarticulate noises. Falstaff, Indiw remembered, had family on Aberdeen. That had to be a little like being landed there. Aberdeen wasn't at all far from here, and it wasn't heavily settled enough to have much in the way of orbital defenses. Sinaha, being a newly opened world, had even less.

"From their com chatter, we learned that it was a detachment from one of these three swarms, a detachment *not* escorting a Breeder, that destroyed *Katukin*. Another whole swarm, which *is* escorting a Breeder, is even now attacking *Katular*.

"If they get by *Katular,* they'll go for Sinaha—a very sparsely settled Ardr colony." *Where I had hoped to become landed.* "If they establish their Breeder there, Tier treaty with the Hyos requires us to surrender the entire planet to them."

"We know," said Falstaff. "Go on."

"The two other swarms, headed for Aberdeen, attacked *Tacoma,* destroyed all defending fighters, and boarded—I'm not sure how. They've brought two Breeders aboard. Those Breeders are, even now, on two different flight decks, ready for instant launch. We couldn't get a clue as to what's keeping the two swarms from annihilating each other.

"Capturing a carrier is another unique innovation. And so's this. They intend to use *Tacoma* to elude Aberdeen's planetary defenses and take up close orbit. They'll launch their own ships and be down on the ground before anyone knows what's really happening. And the planet will be theirs. They'll have the right to kill any non-Hyos found on the surface after they've officially announced possession. If they get both

Aberdeen and Sinaha, that will move the border. And it's all legal—in the treaty."

There was complete silence. Even the ill and wounded stopped coughing and groaning. Feet stopped shuffling.

Someone said, "It's unimaginable. Hyos *never* vary their methods!"

Someone else answered, "A species doesn't get to dominate a planet without having learned from failure. For decades, they've been singularly unsuccessful broaching our frontier. I think the Hyos have finally noticed that and have begun to learn again while we've been getting complacent."

Falstaff said, "What's really interesting is that the Hyos establishment didn't warn us about this alliance of swarms. They tipped us to a couple of big swarms gathering and gave us permission to attack them on the surface of their own planets, yet neglected to mention this. Does it signal a new policy?"

"Commander Falstaff," mused someone back by the wounded, "did it seem to you like the planetary strike you went on was a well-engineered trap? After all, only four of you came back from that one."

Indiw said, "While my wing was off *Katukin* on a similar planetary strike, *Katukin* was destroyed. We encountered more ground resistance than usual on that strike, too."

Falstaff shrugged. "If it is a change in policy, then we'll just change to accommodate them."

That got a rise out of the people, but a very quiet one since there could be Hyos anywhere, listening.

By the next morning, they numbered twenty able-bodied combatants and a couple dozen wounded. The mobile wounded cared for the disabled and did whatever else they could to support the effort.

Falstaff was still the ranking officer present. He, Indiw, and Chancy were the only pilots.

The Hyos had exterminated all those in the hospital. They held and guarded the key control areas of the ship. From the engine sound, the ship was already heading for Aberdeen.

If they were going to do anything, it would have to be within the next few hours. But they had only twenty to overcome hundreds of Hyos spread through miles and miles of corridors.

If the situation weren't so grave, Indiw would have been fascinated watching the humans discuss possible tactics. As it was, he just wished somebody had a viable idea. Someone provided cups and started to pour hot drinks for everyone.

They weren't being deliberately offensive. In fact, several had apologized to him. And they had strung tarps to try to provide him privacy for his own needs. So Indiw kept a tight leash on himself. The human habits—and odors—had to be endured. It wouldn't be long. They would all be dead within a few hours.

"Indiw," said Falstaff suddenly. "Do Hyos smell? I mean can you detect a distinctly Hyos body odor?"

"I don't know. Some Ardr can. It's been described by Ardr diplomats who had to deal with them. But some Ardr can't detect the odor."

"Can they smell us?"

Could anything alive not smell them? He didn't say it aloud. Humans were sensitive about their odor. "I don't know. But the whole ship smells of human. A slight increase from proximity of a few individuals might not be very noticeable."

"Can Hyos smell Ardr?"

"No. That was established early in the first negotiations." *And made everything much harder.*

Osgood asked, "What are you thinking, Commander?"

Chancy said with the air of the suddenly enlightened, "He's thinking that we've been going at this all wrong. There's no way we can recapture this ship. And we could *never* hold it.

But we don't have to. All we really can do is call for help, and if that help blows *Tacoma* out of space, well—so? We all accepted the dangers before we signed on. The point isn't that we survive. The point is that Aberdeen and the Tier border survive. Agreed?"

Falstaff nodded. "Grim as it seems, I think that's the only way to look at this problem."

Everyone but Indiw agreed. Indiw had begun to see this as a chance to drive home his claim to a parcel of land on Sinaha. After his battle in space, and now this, who wouldn't want such a proven defender as a neighbor? And if it took cooperating with humans to counter the Hyos's new tactic, well, we all make sacrifices for land. But he couldn't afford to become the sole survivor of this battle. Not again. Or his argument would never stick.

Falstaff waved a piece of ration cake as he spoke with gestures. "A couple of good circuitry wizards burrowing through the correct bulkhead, and a few accomplished cat burglars could take control of this ship.

"Now we couldn't hold it for more than a few minutes. But we don't have to. All we have to do is yell, and we'll have done our job. After that, if we can manage to cripple *Tacoma* to slow the Hyos down, so much the better. You with me, Indiw?"

Falstaff's tone was rhetorical, and he rushed on to explain his idea, sketching on the deck with the bitten tip of his ration bar. "I was a carrier pilot before I took to the fighters. You see, everything this ship does funnels through the central memory core. They know that, and will have guards thick as flies here, here, and here.

"But do they know that with a handful of replacement circuit boards and some chips we could divert all functions to the backup brain without getting anywhere near the central core? Will they be guarding the backup brain? That's where Indiw's nose comes in." He finally looked at Indiw. "You don't seem convinced. What's the problem?"

Wizards were obviously clergy, and he wasn't about to open *that* subject with humans. And since a pit bull wasn't bovine, he was sure a cat burglar wasn't feline. So he asked, "What's a cat burglar?"

Everyone laughed. "He means we'll have to get onto the bridge via a long, dangerous, and difficult climb up a maintenance tube, and we'll have to do it quietly."

"I understand."

"Now," started Falstaff.

But Indiw interrupted as the implications sank in, "Walt, doesn't *Tacoma* have a Winslow Security System protecting the bridge controls?" Surely all Tier carriers did.

Chancy said, "Yes, but to take the bridge, the Hyos had to disable that."

"They'll have reinstated it," said Indiw. "There are two swarms here. They don't trust one another, and they know there must be human survivors around somewhere. They'll have armed guards *and* the Winslow will be operating. There's no way intruders could get through that shield and at the controls."

Someone said, "The Hyos did it."

Osgood explained, "They took out the backup power and gutted the fail-safes. Someone among them had some knowledge of Tier design, enough I think to repair most of the damage they've done if they wanted to."

Everyone looked at him. He added, "I did a short stint in Engineering before I decided on a purser's career."

Falstaff said, "So, the Winslows are just another problem to be overcome by the cat burglar team. The whole scheme is useless if Indiw can't tell us whether Hyos are—or have recently been—in the backup brain compartment. And he'll have to do that without actually going in. If this is to work, we have to preserve the element of surprise at all costs. We can't afford risks until the very last minute.

"After we know what Indiw can—or can't—contribute, then we can plan our assault accordingly. If the Hyos haven't been into the backup brain, all we have to do is cut our way in and take over control. If they have, we'll have to dispose of the guards first, then check for booby traps, *then* take over control. If he can't tell us, we'll have to prepare as if there's a regiment in there, which is bad because we'll need all our best fighters up top—especially if we have to deal with the Winslow.

"I'm not too worried about the Winslow. If the Hyos could do it, so can we. Besides, if we come up with something innovative, we can sell it to the Winslow Corporation and we'll all be rich!

"The wizards who tackle the backup brain won't have long to work. They'll have to be ready by the time the cat burglars reach the bridge. But the wizards can't start too soon because the bridge crew must not get word that there are humans into mischief at the backup brain before the cat burglars get there to distract them."

A medic offered, "Hyos keel over real fast when exposed to formaldehyde fumes. We've got enough to flood a small compartment, but not the main bridge. Course it's toxic to humans, too, but we can stand it better than they. Lots better, especially if we can get hold of some more filter masks. Ardr think it's a condiment! I won't vouch for what it might do to circuitry boards."

"Interesting." Falstaff's eyes were suddenly bright.

"But," objected Indiw, "*Tacoma* has no external communications at all. How can we signal anyone?"

"We're getting close to Aberdeen. If they're planning to approach without rousing suspicion, they'll have the com repaired by now. Or at least in a few hours from now. They won't know the drills and signs for a silent approach as a friendly vessel. They haven't had time to dig them out from under the Captain's security lock. So they'll fix the com. So we can use it."

Osgood rose. "I think I can find out if they've fixed it yet. The sooner we do this, the better chance someone else has of stopping *Tacoma* from making orbit." At Falstaff's nodded permission, he picked his way over seated figures and went out into the maintenance passage pulling a ration bar out of his hip pocket as he went.

"So that's the plan," finished Falstaff. "Unless someone has a better idea?" After a moment of silence, Falstaff stood and began picking out people and assigning them to jobs. Falstaff didn't know most of these people so there was considerable discussion about which ones had which skills. It was interesting how not one of them ever just volunteered and went and did something.

Falstaff set up a timetable for the operation, which Chancy dubbed Operation Up Theirs, adding, "And our squadron names are Cat Burglar and Wizard. If they do overhear us on a com channel, they'll *never* get it!"

Everyone laughed but Indiw. He set bewilderment aside when one of the walking wounded called him over to ask technical questions about com circuits. It was the woman Falstaff had assigned to create a com channel for them and find communicators they could carry. Their com channel had to be Hyos-proof, and very reliable.

Outwardly Indiw cooperated, but inwardly he was appalled. Every one of the humans seemed to be infected with the enthusiasm one might bring to a game played out on a neutral walkway, not the grim realities they all faced now.

"Indiw? Prepared to go nosing around?" It was Falstaff, wiping his hands on a damp towel and grinning.

At Indiw's blank look, he translated, "To find out if you can smell Hyos."

"Oh. Just let me take my boots off."

"Take your boots off?"

His sandals were probably still in his quarters behind Hyos guards in the little travel bag. Or worse yet, had been discarded by some Hyos trespasser. That thought hardened his anger as he struggled with the boots. "In case we run into any serious opposition. I hate being hampered in a fight."

By then he had one boot off and was flexing his toe claws luxuriously while he worked on the other's catch.

Falstaff said, "Oh. I see. Certainly."

Indiw made a couple of experimental lunges to test the deck traction, leaning back and stretching into a kick at the end of the second. People shrank from him in alarm. He resumed a normal stance. "Ready."

Chancy said, gaze fixed on Indiw's feet, "Walt, don't take any chances."

Falstaff went over and applied his lips to hers, then said something quietly into her ear. She punched him in the ribs and turned away. Indiw wondered what the human male mortality rate must be, if they all had as poor judgment as Falstaff when it came to sensing a female's choice. Of course, with virtually no sense of smell, what chance did a human male have? At least when she struck him a warning blow, he did have sense enough to retreat and she was polite enough not to pursue.

Falstaff circled wide around Indiw, eyeing his toe claws with what could only be envy, and led the way out into the darker maintenance corridor. "You do much unarmed combat training?"

"About average." Indiw raised his goggles, not commenting that he expected to be much better by the time he made his first land challenge.

"Ardr average is rather high by human standards. Ever killed anyone with those claws?"

"Yes." He glanced at the human. Was he being judgmental? No. It wasn't Falstaff's way. Indiw said, "You know it's impossible for an Ardr to reach adulthood without surviving mortal combat, dozens of times."

"Reading about it is one thing. Seeing it is something else. You really don't have parents. Or relatives? No concept of family at all?"

"Relatives are something I've only read about. I thought I understood. But watching you and Chancy, I realize I don't. You said you have family on Aberdeen."

"Yes. That makes Aberdeen special to me. Like home. What's Chancy got to do with it?"

"She is not to be the bearer of your new children?"

Falstaff made a strangled sound and his face darkened. Before Indiw could become unduly alarmed, Falstaff said, "It hasn't gone that far yet." Under his breath, he added something that sounded like "I don't think."

"What would be different if it had?" Seeing Falstaff's expression, he knew he was treading on dangerous ground. "It's just that I keep thinking that everything I don't understand about humans hinges on this mysterious capacity. Sexuality is generally viewed as such an unimportant area that there isn't much written information in the texts on humans. And over the last few days, I've begun to wonder if what is there is correct."

"Oh. I see. Well. I've known Marla for about a year, and that's not really long enough to decide to make a lifetime commitment to someone."

"Is that why she keeps rejecting you?"

"Rejecting me?"

"Hitting you to make you retreat."

"Hitting me?"

Indiw retracted his claws and made as good an imitation of a human fist as he could, then touched the backs of his knuckles to Falstaff's upper arm. "Like that."

"Oh! That's not rejection. It's acceptance."

It is?

"It's a gesture that conveys a lot of different meanings depending on context. We—understand each other."

"This is not sufficient to make a relative of her?" Indiw couldn't imagine any higher qualification for a lifelong association than thinking like another person. After all, how else would one choose one's neighbors so as not to be surrounded by people you wanted to kill every time you were forced to cooperate with them?

"No. It's not sufficient." Falstaff dragged a hand along a bulkhead as if he were scent-marking it, then drove his fist into it. But then he kept moving. "Well, to be perfectly honest, I have thought about it once in a while. It's just—too soon. She hasn't even met my family yet."

"On Aberdeen? Do you own land there?"

"No, I don't. I really don't like the place very much. But it's their home, and they're all I have left. I'll probably retire there, just to be near them, and I've no idea how Marla might like the place—or my relatives!"

"Relatives always like each other?"

Falstaff paused to stare at him a moment, thoughtful. Then he resumed their cautious trek. "Not—always. But I like mine. I want to watch my nieces and nephews grow up and have kids of their own. I can see my brother in the eldest boy already. That's the most incredible sensation, to look at a boy and see the man he will be."

They reached a point where they had to converse in very quiet whispers. "I don't understand."

"They're my brother's children. My brother and I had the same mother and the same father. I don't have any children. So my brother's children may be all of me that will live on after me. It's like they're my own children. Doesn't that mean anything to you?"

"I can't imagine what it would be like." Indiw thought about the lovely, moist glade where he'd hatched. At least he presumed he had. He didn't remember the event, though he'd watched other eggs hatch there.

His earliest memory was triumphantly disemboweling a competitor who tried to steal his first kill. He'd eaten the rich organs of both the animal and his competitor, and few had dared challenge him after that. But his most treasured memory was puzzling out the lock on the gate and emerging from the hatchery into the real world. "How do you decide which of those children is worthy to survive?"

Falstaff paused at an intersection and stared at Indiw.

Indiw made an apologetic gesture. "I never found any reference to it, maybe because it's too private—"

"No. I just keep forgetting there's no way we'll ever understand each other. Indiw, human parents accept whatever children are born to them. Survival selection is done way before birth, simply by choosing the other parent carefully."

"Is there something wrong with Commander Chancy's genes?"

"No! Besides, when there is a genetic problem it's corrected before conception. We do the best we can, and when it doesn't work, we accept the individual child and try to help overcome the problems we have caused by creating that child. No person is unworthy to survive."

"Oh, I didn't mean that a *person* could be unworthy, only a child."

Falstaff looked upward, walked around in a little circle, then came back close enough to whisper, "We regard our children as the most worthy to survive of all. They are our posterity, our future. They are what we live *for*. And, if necessary, what we die for."

All of his abstract understanding of what he'd read fell together in Indiw's mind. "You mean, because you know which ones carry your *own* genes?"

Falstaff grinned. "Yes! And when you know what it feels like to love your own child, you know what others have to go through if a child of theirs is hurt or lost. Every adult is a child who had a mother and a father. It's a common experience that welds all humanity together regardless of culture or planet of origin."

"I see." He digested that for a few moments, dizzy with the implications, but coming back to the problem of understanding Falstaff's relationship with Chancy. "Then it really wouldn't do if you were to choose Commander Chancy and she took as violent a hatred to your brother's children as she has to me. Do you really think that's a character trait of hers and not just a result of my making an enemy of her?"

"Indiw, she doesn't hate you. She's just a little xenophobic from time to time, but she's getting over it. She put you up for the Croninwet, after all."

"*That's* what I mean!"

"Indiw, she didn't know it would ruin your career. She thought we were dead. Everybody thought so."

"Fine thing to do to the dead!"

Falstaff stopped, the palm of his right hand holding his forehead. Then he turned and said, "Indiw, listen carefully. The Croninwet is usually given posthumously. The money's supposed to go to your surviving relatives—people who depended on your earning power for their food and shelter."

All his nebulous enlightenment vanished. He really didn't understand humans—not at all. How could one person depend on another for food and shelter? "You mean, Commander Chancy put you up for the Croninwet because she was thinking of your sister's children not having food and shelter?"

"No!" Then Falstaff looked thoughtful. "But she knew my pay was going into their college fund."

College-fund. Indiw decided that if he lived through all this, he'd have to take a refresher in Tier standard with emphasis in human dialects. They made compound words that didn't mean what either component did. "Well, if you're certain she doesn't hate me, I'll have to reevaluate."

"She doesn't hate you. She just doesn't trust you. She knows enough about Ardr to know you have a very different attitude toward killing than we do, and she knows that Ardr don't form bonds the way we do. If you got upset enough, she thinks you just might kill me, which would make her feel—" He broke off and stared at the overhead shadows.

Indiw prompted, "She doesn't think killing you would be difficult?" Considering the negligent way she treated Falstaff, her power must be astonishing.

"She's not sure it would be difficult *enough.*"

"Are you? Sure?"

"Pretty much."

"That's about how I'd measured it. You can tell her—I may not be trustworthy by her standards, but I'm not stupid." Then he signaled Falstaff to lead the way onward.

The human whispered, "Threlkeld found us a spot in Engineering that we can get to without being seen. There are always Hyos there. If you can detect the Hyos in Engineering, we'll check out the backup brain."

They came to another intersection and turned into a way that was low, dark, and narrow. They had to crawl through and climb a short tube to another maintenance hatch. Falstaff pointed to a softly luminescent sign. ENGINEERING. It was followed by a string of coordinates.

The hatch above them had an open grill, designed to drain fluids when the repair bay was in use. Beneath them, a control plate was set to apply a gravity draw on the waste fluid. Falstaff squatted down and held out his interlaced hands. "Step up. I think you're tall enough to reach the grill."

Mindful of his toe claws, Indiw planted his foot on the human's warm, slightly damp palms, controlled the reflexive flinch, and stepped up. Falstaff rose to his full height, but it wasn't enough. "Hold still," he breathed as he stepped up onto the human's shoulders. He was just tall enough to sniff the air wafting down from the repair bay.

Machine oil. Burned components. Human sweat. Human vomit, blood, and excrement. People had died up there. Heated power tools. Cool, reprocessed air. And something else.

He sniffed. It was something he'd never smelled before. Not unpleasant, but vaguely threatening.

He took another long minute to examine the odor. He got two more good whiffs of the pungency, and finally remembered the description the diplomats had written of the odor. *Hyos!*

Indiw climbed down Falstaff's body, nodded, and led off into the crawlway. When they'd retreated to a point where they could whisper, Indiw said, "Yes, I can smell them."

"You're sure?"

"It's odd that one person can write a description of an odor that makes no sense to another until presented with that very same odor. But recognition is indisputable."

"If you say so. All right, let's get down to the backup brain." They had to consult a map three times, retracing their steps once, but eventually they found the right room and ended up curled into a tiny space beside a ventilation uptake from the backup brain's operations room.

Using a power tool, Falstaff silently opened an access hatch into the side of the duct, a hatch that was no more than a hand span across from claw tip to claw tip. Wind raced wildly in the duct, and the sound changed when the access opened.

They waited, listening hard. Had any Hyos noticed the changed sound? Nothing. Falstaff nodded.

When he took his goggles off, Indiw was just able to insert most of his face into the duct, though his horns wouldn't fit. The sound changed again. But now he was intent on the air rushing past. Light from the room played on his closed eyelids. He searched and searched for the telltale odor. Nothing. He pulled out.

With his lips close to Falstaff's ear, he whispered, "If they've been here, they're long, long gone. I don't think any of them has ever been in there, at least not in anything less than full vacuum gear."

Falstaff nodded, a single hard jerk of his head. Then he replaced the access panel and together they scrambled back to the main corridor. There, Indiw sniffed.

Now that he'd been sensitized to it, he could pick out Hyos odor easily. "Hyos have passed this way. Recently."

"It's the only way the map shows back to base."

They went on cautiously.

"Wait!" whispered Indiw. "Hyos! Coming toward us."

Falstaff looked about. They were in a long tunnel hung with pipes and strewn with neatly sheathed bundles of wires, the manual control panels. There was a narrow, dark space above the pipes. Too narrow to hide in. They raced back the way they'd come, but they hadn't passed any concealment.

At a junction, Falstaff darted down the darker branch and paused. Here the maintenance tunnel became a bare shaft, an access crawlway into something. Indiw didn't know what. He was lost.

"We're going to have to kill them if they come this way," whispered Falstaff.

Indiw loosened his clothing and flexed his claws. The humans hadn't been able to lay hands on any weapons that didn't make too much noise or energy to be noticed, so they were unarmed. But the Hyos were heavily armed.

"Any idea how many there are?"

"Two, I think." He was thinking longingly of the weapon he'd seen Chancy demolishing a target with—blindfolded. It was silent, and undetectable by modern security. It would have been perfect. Of course, a good jungle knife would have done just as well if the Hyos were not in armor.

Falstaff grinned. There was no humor in it. "Only two? Then we've got the advantage!"

They heard the Hyos then, rattling battle gear, pausing, shining their lights everywhere, talking nervously. The only word Indiw could pick out was their version of *human*.

And then a shaft of light struck him. Hyos light. Indiw went for the source of it, smashed the arm holding the light with one kick, twisted in midair, landed continuing his turn, and sank two claws into the Hyos's eye sockets.

Blood spurted around Indiw's fingers, but he didn't check his movement. He went down with the body, extracted his claws, and rolled end for end away from his victim looking for the next attacker.

A blinding shaft of energy sizzled into the blood on his victim's chest, right where his body would have been had he not kept moving. Falstaff lay dazed against one wall. Indiw whirled into another kick sequence, missed the first contact, but connected hard with the second. The Hyos's gun flew off in an arc and clattered noisily into a pipe. But it didn't go off. The Hyos fumbled for his com unit while Indiw completed his recovery move.

Falstaff was on his feet. Indiw, continuing his movement, looped one elbow around the Hyos's neck and pulled backward in a move his instructor had assured him would kill a Hyos.

There was no breaking sound, and the Hyos only yelled. Indiw shifted his grip and with one hand yanked at a wire he hoped was the Hyos com unit's connection. Then he danced out of reach of the remarkably flexible arms and legs. Falstaff had the dead Hyos's gun. He fired at the live Hyos.

Predictably, the armor deflected the weapon's field. It splashed into a bulkhead and melted a spot. The Hyos went for Falstaff. But Indiw was behind the Hyos, and by the light of the discharge, he spotted the armor's couplings where the chest piece joined in the back. He lunged, yanked, twisted, and then grabbed the Hyos's armor by the crotch and the neck and heaved.

Falstaff saw the unshelled Hyos coming toward him and crouched. Indiw decanted the Hyos out of his body armor. The Hyos rolled over Falstaff's back, and onto the floor. Indiw heaved the breastplate aside while Falstaff calmly shot the Hyos through the middle.

The body collapsed with a smoking, stinking hole in it.

Indiw's toe claws ached with thwarted anticipation. It was probably just as well he hadn't gutted the Hyos. There would have been a lot of purple blood. As it was, even the other one had died so fast he hadn't bled much.

Falstaff leaned on the long stock of the gun, panting. Indiw wiped his claws on the armor's lining and retracted them. "I guess you were right. We did have the advantage."

Falstaff just grinned. "Help me get the bodies up that crawlway. I think it leads to the food processing plant."

Bending, Indiw hesitated and looked up at Falstaff, rejected the obvious interpretation of his remark—there were, after all, treaty conventions even with Hyos—and picked up the legs by the hocks while Falstaff took the shoulders.

Together they got the corpses up the side shaft and found a heavily insulated hatch into a refrigerated space. It was filled with packaged food. They buried both bodies in a pile of containers, and Falstaff said, "Remind me, if we get out of this, to be sure somebody comes for these two."

"I will." He was ashamed anything else had ever occurred to him.

Carrying the two weapons, they made their way back to the command center of Operation Up Theirs. Their news galvanized the humans into a more feverish pitch.

After considerable discussion with the others, Falstaff assigned Indiw to the Cat Burglar Squad. He got to work with the humans creating the assault plan. At one point Falstaff said, "Well, that about wraps it up, except for the Winslows. Indiw, you brought the problem up. How do you suggest we handle it?"

They were huddled over a schematic of the bridge, focusing their attention on the maintenance hatch they would use for entry. Indiw scraped a claw in an arc in front of the hatch. "Is this about where the Winslow screen would cut?"

"Yeah," said Falstaff. "About three feet from the bulkhead. It's a force screen that learns genetic patterns. If you haven't been authorized, you can't get through it. Energy weapons won't penetrate it. Missile weapons bounce back at you. Remember how you got me onto the *Katular* bridge? The Captain had to argue the system into passing a human through."

Indiw skewered the symbol for the correct console. "The Winslow is controlled from here?"

"Right."

He measured the distance with two claws, and suddenly knew the answer. "Commander Chancy, I must make a—difficult confession."

"Confession? What could you have done?"

He hoped she had the necessary self-control to hear this. "I accidentally entered the gym area when you were hard centering using a device shaped like this." He sketched a picture of the primitive weapon. He wasn't going to mention that he'd seen how many times she'd missed her target.

"The long bow? Yes. What did you do wrong?"

"I was there. I saw you destroy your target."

"The target range is a public area, Indiw. You could stand around and watch all day and nobody would care."

He squirmed his astonishment aside. "I have used a weapon resembling the 'long bow,' though without your success. It projects a low-speed missile with no onboard electronics of any sort. It doesn't even have as much electric field as a living body. Its only genetic trace is plant material. Such a missile would pass through a Winslow field without hindrance."

"*Oh—my—God!*" Falstaff stared at the bridge schematic, then at Chancy. There was a long, still silence as he stared at her with no expression on his features and the other humans glanced at one another with worried frowns. Finally, Osgood said, "She'd have to go in first."

Falstaff nodded, a strange jerky movement. But then all the humans started breathing, and he asked, "Marla, can you hit a one-inch target at—oh, what is it—three yards, four maybe? Penetrate that housing—skewer the control board—it'd take an impact of—what? Anybody guess?"

Several engineers began arguing specs on the console components. Marla supplied the velocity of her *arrows* at launch. Engineers calculated, and a chorus of whoops went up, quiet, whispered whoops. Everyone was acutely mindful of the Hyos everywhere, especially since the encounter Indiw and Falstaff had had in the maintenance passages.

Two of the walking wounded, physical training experts knowledgeable in that part of the ship, departed to stage a quick raid on the target range with Marla's instructions about which arrows to bring. Meanwhile two amateur artisans who were immobilized by their wounds began fabricating a new tip for one of her arrows, a tip that would pass the Winslow field and yet be hard and sharp enough to bore through the housing material at the velocity she could deliver.

Indiw began to doubt the wisdom of the plan. They all knew she'd only have time for one shot. If Marla were internally off-center, she could easily miss as he'd seen her do. If she missed, they'd be dead.

On the other hand, he told himself, this time she wouldn't be blind. Humans relied a lot on their eyes since they had no nose to speak of, not to mention their faulty hearing. He had once wondered how such creatures could have risen to dominate a planet. Fighting with humans, he'd begun to see how they made up for each other's weaknesses, creating a very formidable pack. That trait might just serve them well in this situation—if Marla Chancy wasn't too stressed out to make her shot.

While they waited for the gym raiding party to return, Indiw took advantage of a moment when no one was watching him to retire to his private area for a hasty squat. Inevitably, it proved to be a difficult passage because he'd been on a steady diet of ration bars.

He had barely begun when the tarp forming the wall of his retreat right beside him bent inward and molded into the shape of two bodies entwined. Voices, low murmurs that were barely an arm's length from him, caught him in an awkward condition. He couldn't move. Though he knew he shouldn't listen, he couldn't help it.

"Marla, we've got to settle this."

"I thought it was settled. You're keeping your Ardr and I'm flying the g'ddamned S&R missions."

"You know why I didn't want you on my wing, or even in my squadron?"

"Because you don't think I'm good enough. Because you don't trust me in a fight. Because you prefer your hotshot Ardr."

"Indiw has nothing to do with this. It's because I'm a coward. I can't face the idea of the pain—if I lost you. I finally saw it when I flashed on a vision of you standing up to a bridge full of Hyos with nothing but a bow and arrow!

You're the best marksman in this fleet. You're the best one—you're the *only* one for this job, and it's our only chance. It's Aberdeen's only chance—all on one bow shot. How could you say I don't trust you in a fight?"

"If you could see another way, you'd take it. You're in command here. You'd order me to stay behind with the wounded if you could justify it."

"Marla, why would that be so bad?"

"To be helpless while others fight for my survival? You've *got* to be kidding!"

"Is that all it is? Fear of helplessness? Fear of owing your life to another?"

"It's not *fear*. . . ."

"Hell it's not. *Look* at it, Marla. Be honest with yourself. Be honest with me."

The two forms melted together. In the throes of elimination, Indiw could only stare helplessly at the writhing shape just inches from his nose. And he was thankful when, a moment later, it became clear they would make no more than another teasing contact, the kind they apparently permitted in public.

"Well? Why is it you want to be wherever I am? To be in the thick of the most dangerous action? Isn't there a lot of action like that almost anywhere you can think of? Do you have to follow me around to get into a good fight?"

"Oh, Walt. . . ." Her breathing filled with a liquid burbling for a moment, then an arhythmic gasping that throttled back swiftly to silence. "I want to be there to protect you—or to die with you."

"And I want you to be way, way behind me, back home, back at the place I'm out here to keep safe for you—and my children. Marla, you idiot, we should have gotten married months ago!"

"Now that's ridiculous. I'm not going to give up my career, and certainly not to marry you. All we ever do is fight."

"Because we don't listen to each other—or to ourselves, deep inside. I keep saying, in all kinds of veiled ways that I didn't even understand myself, that I don't want you to share my danger, and you keep saying you can't stand to pace around and wait for orders to come mop up my pieces off the starscape.

"Marla, you want to be there to protect me, and I want to protect you by keeping you away. It's a classic. We've both read it in all the texts and still didn't recognize it when we were living it. But it's the stupidest argument mankind has ever invented. I wouldn't let anybody do to me what I want to do to you; you wouldn't let anybody do to you what you want to do to me."

"And what do I want to do to you that's so awful?"

"Distract me in a fight. Slap me in the face with my worst, most primal fears just at the moment my life and the lives of my squadron mates depend on my concentration."

"You're right. I'd never let anybody do that to me."

"So you see? We're two of a kind. We belong together."

"It's not possible."

"Why not?"

Feeling on the verge of success, Indiw had to hold his breath against the gathering grunt that would betray him and disturb the two humans.

"I'm a fighter pilot. I got my first orbital papers when I was fourteen. I flew stunts for Rigby's Circus for two years, and then I was a professional asteroid miner by the time I was sixteen. On my eighteenth birthday, I got my commercial license and signed on with Grosset Tours. I won the Australian Invitational with Raymond Grosset's personal yacht. I won the Terran Open with my own racer.

"But all that was just marking time, waiting to be old enough to sign on as a fighter pilot and fight Hyos. I'm a *professional* pilot here by choice just like you, not a draftee doing time waiting to be sent home. Just like you, I always have been a pilot. I always will be. *That's* why I want to fly with you. The sex is so good, the flying just has to be better. Falling in love with you just complicated matters. Marrying you wouldn't solve anything. Then they'd *never* let us fly together."

"So you are in love with me."

"Yes, dammit."

"So what should we do about it?"

"Pretend it's not there and maybe it'll go away?"

"Not sound psychology. We're both pilots, both top pilots. And neither of us is so young anymore. If we get out of this alive, someone will have the bright idea that we ought to be promoted into desk jobs."

"Then I'll resign and find something else to fly. But I'll always fly."

"We could use the Croninwet money to found our own transport company—based on Aberdeen. In a few years, when we've had time to expand, my nephews will be old enough to fly for us. What do you think? You have the contacts, I have the money. What say we teach the Hyos not to mess with human transport ships?"

"You're crazy."

"You don't like that idea? Well, what say we build a couple of racers and parlay the stake into a real fortune? Then we can hire some people to build us a transport company."

"Three years' pay wouldn't go far building a racer."

"No, but we both have reputations on the racing circuit. Once we were in, backers would rally round with money-stars in their eyes. I've always wanted to try the Olympic Relays, but I could never find a partner I wouldn't be dragging every inch of the way. Now I've found one, I don't want to let her go. You don't have to marry me until you feel like it, but meanwhile, we could fly together without risking all our buddies and maybe a planet or two on a moment's distraction."

There was a long silence in which the form against the tarp writhed slowly. "You mean this kind of distraction?"

"Yeah. '*Tacoma* Control, we have ignition!' "

"So I notice. Hmmmm."

"Say yes, Marla."

"Yes. At the first threat of a desk job, yes. But not before."

"Deal."

"Walt?"

"Hmmm?"

"Not here, Walt."

"Hmmm? Oh. Right."

The form separated into two and vanished from the tarp. As soon as he could no longer hear their steps, Indiw loosed the grunt he'd been suppressing and achieved his purpose. Panting, he sagged, his mind racing to evaluate what he'd overheard while his sense of propriety set his horns to burning. Two times they'd actually wanted privacy, and he intruded on them—and them on him—because of the way humans designed their ships.

When Indiw emerged from his violated sanctum, he found the humans busily preparing for the assault. There was an easy cheer among them, a kind of subtle flow of body language that hadn't been there a few minutes before. It was almost like watching an experienced Ardr wing breaking into battle maneuvers.

Falstaff was at one end of the pattern and Chancy at the other, but the weave seemed to be stretched between them. It was a most incredible phenomenon to observe, and he wondered if he'd have noticed if he hadn't overheard their private interaction. He suddenly began to believe that they could succeed, and that there was a chance they might even live through it all. There was that much magic in the air. Perhaps it had something to do with the clergymen assigned to take over the backup brain.

Soon, the gym raiders returned with Chancy's equipment, and within a few hours Indiw and the Cat Burglar Squad were climbing an infinitely long ladder in a dark shaft, all of them barefoot and wearing nothing metallic or hard enough to ring against metal except the tools and weapons in their backpacks.

They were climbing a ladder inside a vacuum-tight bulkhead that divided them from the patrolled areas. Occasionally, they clung breathlessly to their ladder rungs and listened to Hyos talking on the other side of that bulkhead, praying to all their various deities that no cat burglar would make a betraying sound.

Indiw had noticed the human feet as they shed their boots. With his curled-up little toes, Falstaff's were uniquely ugly, so maybe that wasn't why humans preferred boots. However, the lack of claws made them all look impotent. And they moved as if their naked feet embarrassed them, so Indiw made sure he wasn't caught looking. Now, every time he had to stop with his eyes a bare clawspan from human feet, his own horns ached with embarrassment for the poor clawless creatures.

Linked to the Cat Burglars by a headset and subvocal microphone that Falstaff carried, the Wizard Squad was already into the backup brain and working.

The Cat Burglars were all shaking in every muscle by the time they paused a good deck shy of the goal to catch their breath and unpack their weapons. Falstaff reported via hand signs that the Wizards were on schedule.

They hung the empty backpacks on the side of the ladder and advanced, slowly and silently, to the bridge level.

The lead on the ladder was a woman with each toe tipped with a blot of bright red as if wishing they were functional claws. She carried their only shield, a riot shield that could fend off Hyos heat weapons, perhaps long enough for Chancy to get off her all-important bow shot. As they reached the access hatch, the shield bearer worked at it with a set of coded keys one of the walking wounded had brought back from a foray.

A moment later she stowed the keys, swung the shield onto her left arm, and gestured ready. Behind her, Chancy settled the nocked bow and arrow in her left hand, found her balance on the rung, and signed ready.

Falstaff, far enough below Chancy to allow her weapon to maneuver, unlimbered the atomizer of formaldehyde slung at his belt and indicated that Wizard was ready. He had one of the Hyos rifles they'd captured slung over his back.

Indiw unslung the second Hyos rifle and signaled his own readiness, and the signal rippled on down the squad. Some of the people also made solemn prayer gestures. Then the lead woman with the pathetic little red toe claws flung the hatch open.

She turned the shield sideways to get it through the hatch, then deployed it and advanced to the edge of the Winslow field. Chancy disappeared through the hatch and Indiw knew she'd be leveling her arrow over the top of the shield, just as he'd seen her practice a few minutes ago.

They didn't wait for her shot, though. Falstaff dove through the hatch, scooting to the right, leaving Indiw room to dive left. The others, he knew, would be scrambling right behind him, so he kept moving.

Chancy's arrow was through the Winslow and arcing toward the target.

The first barrage of Hyos fire hit the riot shield, having no difficulty passing *out* through a Winslow shield. Simultaneously, Falstaff heaved the formaldehyde container into the midst of a thick clump of bare-faced Hyos technicians who were clustered around a console outside the Winslow screen arguing so intensely they hadn't noticed the intruders yet.

Chancy's arrow hit its mark squarely. Sparks flew and the field sizzled green, then vanished.

Another cluster of Hyos techs worked frantically at the main console, also ignoring the intruders. Clearly things had not been going their way even before the assault team arrived on the bridge.

Indiw rolled through the arc that had been the Winslow field and tucked in behind a freestanding console. In perfect synchronization with Falstaff, he fired the Hyos rifle, covering the entry of those behind them on the ladder. Several of the unarmored Hyos techs collapsed from the formaldehyde before the ventilators dissipated it. Some others went down under fire. So far only a few had returned fire.

The humans boiled out of the hatch onto the bridge.

As the Hyos marshaled return fire, Indiw felt the air heating right through his flight suit. He didn't need to raise his faceplate to know the rank odor of human and Hyos blood and the smell of human flesh burning. And he didn't want to smell that together with the appetizing odor of formaldehyde. A bolt burned his left elbow. He kept firing.

Over the central console, an amber tactical display expanded in midair to show a rapidly approaching planetary surface. Aberdeen.

"My God!" grated Chancy, half rising from behind her cover to stare at the tactical display. "The dish! They've targeted the main dish on the southern continent! They could bore a hole right through the mantle."

Even as she spoke, the armored Hyos defenders moved together to form a tightening circle around the main bridge console in the center of the open space, making a wall of Hyos bodies and blazing Hyos weapons.

Beyond them, Indiw could just see a blinking light over a pair of doors on the other side of the bridge. It had to signal a lift arriving. That wasn't in the plan. The woman with the shield, covered by Chancy with a sport-caliber hand beamer, was supposed to have advanced to the main console to jam the doors, and prevent reinforcements from arriving. But they were pinned down by an advancing squad of Hyos.

Taking careful aim through a crack in the Hyos circle of defense, Indiw fired at the doors, but missed. A Hyos went down.

Falstaff scrambled around the edge of the bridge and circled behind Chancy who was laying down a covering fire for him. He took shots at the doors as he moved, but he couldn't get an angle on them. "It's no good." He tossed his rifle to Indiw and snapped, "Cover me," and scooted, half bent over, across the open deck toward the momentary hole the fallen Hyos had left.

Indiw heard Chancy gasp, but she kept firing, calmly picking off armored Hyos guards with what amounted to nothing more than a short-range target pistol. She was probably the only one on the assault squad who could have done any damage with the thing.

Indiw caught Falstaff's weapon with one hand, stood, and bracing each rifle against a hip, he fired them both at once into the circle of armored Hyos around the main console. He got one Hyos whose faceplate was still up, and that one knocked another off balance when he fell.

Paced by the shield woman and Chancy, Indiw advanced firing over Falstaff's bent form as the human stepped on the fallen Hyos and bored through the widening hole Indiw had made in the cordon.

Then Falstaff was through the cordon and at the central console. A beam singed Indiw's left horn right through his helmet. The intense pain doubled him over. Another beam crackled through the space where his head had been.

He dived for cover. The deck where his feet had been vaporized. He rolled and scrambled away and came up behind a chair. Somehow, he'd hung on to one of the weapons.

The bridge doors had begun to open to reveal armored Hyos. Indiw, closer now to the lift doors, fired, heating the doors to discourage the Hyos reinforcements.

The cordon of Hyos had re-formed around the central console, much smaller. Some turned inward to deal with Falstaff while the rest focused fire on Indiw or at the humans who'd taken cover around the bridge.

Indiw wormed around a console, dashed forward, and sprawled behind two human bodies collapsed on one another. The top one was the red-toed woman. Her shield lay on top of her. With one hand, Indiw struggled to get it up while with the other he kept firing at the Hyos converging on Falstaff.

Falstaff shouted success. The amber tactical display twinkled and flashed and Dopplered sounds filled the bridge as *Tacoma*'s main weapon powered down and rotated swiftly away from the planet. The bridge doors closed. Only three of the reinforcements had squeezed through and they were still fumbling with their half-donned armor. They perished in the withering fire laid down by the surviving humans.

Indiw discovered that the heat from the Hyos weapon would penetrate Hyos armor if the contact with the beam was held long enough. He got three more Hyos before a heavy weight landed on his back, and he lost the second weapon.

It was an unarmored Hyos. This time his toe claws drank blood. But there was no time to savor the satisfaction. Several armored Hyos had Falstaff down.

Indiw left the body scrabbling feebly at its entrails and went up and over an intervening console, pushed off from a chair, and launched at the armored figures on Falstaff. He knocked some of them aside, and they fell on top of him. A gun butt rammed into his faceplate bending it until it starred and cracked in front of his nose.

He tried the neck hold again, sure he knew now what he'd done wrong the first time. This time the Hyos neck snapped under his arm. Another Hyos on top of him sizzled into stinking ruin. His toe claws caught in Hyos skin and he ripped at it, reflexively sinking his claws into soft entrails. Heaving the body with the broken neck aside, he grappled with another who rammed the butt of a long weapon into his middle completely paralyzing his breathing.

It was a good death.

When Indiw came to, the firing had ceased. Six humans manned the essential bridge stations. The stench that sifted through his broken faceplate was unbearable, but the smoke was gone. Bodies were strewn, draped, and heaped everywhere.

"Indiw!" called Chancy. "Get up here! I've got *Katular,* but they think I'm pulling a practical joke!"

Dizzy, barely able to breathe for the pain in his middle, Indiw leaned on the com console next to her. She was smudged and singed, with one bloody arm clutched across her chest. On the screen was the image of an Ardr he didn't recognize.

He identified himself and said, "Three swarms have united to move the border. *Tacoma* is under Hyos control, orbiting Aberdeen with two Breeders aboard. There are only a dozen or so humans left, but they intend—"

The screen went blank.

"Come on, let's get out of here! We've done all we can," said Chancy. She dragged him toward the maintenance hatch.

Indiw pulled away. "Where's Falstaff?"

She stopped, looked around bewildered. "He was right there a minute—"

"Marla," said someone, pointing. "He's dead. Let's go!"

Dead!

Her hand on his arm slacked, but she didn't move.

"Are you sure?" asked Indiw. He stumbled toward the pile of Hyos bodies he'd crawled out from under. Falstaff's foot, easily recognizable by the oddly shaped small toes, stuck out.

Indiw bent and seized the foot. The leg came away from the pile very easily, dangling free in his grasp. Indiw stood holding the foot, eye following up the calf, up the thigh, and up to the hip, ending in a slant of pelvic bone protruding from a charred mess. Falstaff had been sliced in two by a heat beam.

Chancy made an indescribable sound.

Indiw dropped the leg, staggering back, unable to breathe.

Someone called, "Come on, Commander Indiw, here comes the Hyos cavalry." The lift doors were slowly melting. "Marla!"

But Indiw couldn't move. His eyes wouldn't release Falstaff's foot.

Two humans grabbed his arms and shoved him back toward the maintenance hatch, their only exit. Someone else was dragging Chancy, though she fought them mindlessly.

Someone had rigged a cable inside the hatch, and by plan there should be a crash field deployed at the bottom of the shaft in case they had to jump.

As they waited their turn at the hatch, Chancy broke away and flew at Indiw, her hands closing on his neck, her unexpected weight crashing him to the deck. She bashed the back of his helmet against the deck plates, punctuating her screaming accusations, "Why didn't you hold him back until I could clear a path for him? Why didn't you watch his rear? Why did you let him depend on you—you—you—"

Someone pulled her off, and Indiw, dazed and dizzy, bewildered by the anguished flood of emotion and the singularly ineffectual attack from such a formidable enemy, lunged to his feet, staggering as half his abused muscles refused to obey him.

At that moment, without warning, the deck shook. The air reverberated with new sounds. Everything tilted crazily, then gravity quit. Indiw and his escort drifted several feet off the deck for long seconds, then gravity came back at double normal, slamming Indiw down across a console at an awkward angle, Chancy and another human on top of him.

CHAPTER
EIGHT

★

INDIW DRIFTED TO CONSCIOUSNESS AWARE OF THE FINE mist of healing sap enveloping his skin. Everything hurt. Even breathing hurt. It hurt his chest to inflate his lungs. The air hurt his nose. He could hardly smell anything.

But he wasn't dead.

That's all he knew the first time. Next time, things hurt less. He woke with a clear mind, and the vivid memory of Falstaff's leg. And the mighty puzzle of Chancy's mindless attack.

There was someone standing over him. His nose told him it was Fikkhor, the medic who had been at his Interview. He opened one eye to confirm that. It was true. He was on *Katular,* in the hospital.

"*Tacoma*? What happened?"

"We found you among a lot of dead bodies on the bridge. The humans thought you were dead, too. They've no idea how tough an Ardr can be."

"How did you get onboard? I was sure you'd have to blow the ship up to stop those two swarms." He sat up. "You *did* stop them, didn't you?"

"Just barely." The medic pushed him back down on the sand again and began sponging an oily medicament over his hide.

Every instinct howling outrage, Indiw didn't resist. He couldn't. Everything still hurt, though not as much. It crossed his mind that medics had the most dangerous profession of all and truly earned their land. Then he had to know. "And the other swarm—they didn't get Sinaha?"

"No."

"How come you were here so fast?"

"When our fighters routed them, we chased that swarm because someone figured it had been intending to destroy *Katular,* not just squeeze by us. We got them, but we took a lot of damage. We were so close to Aberdeen by then, we decided to put in here for repairs. We were very close when we got your call. Totaled the main engines getting to *Tacoma* in time, though. We'll be here awhile. Three Fornak carriers are moving in to cover the hole the Hyos made in our line."

Indiw remembered how agitated the Hyos bridge crew had been even before the assault began. No wonder if they'd detected *Katular* approaching. And no wonder they'd deployed *Tacoma*'s big dish and focused it on Aberdeen. He said as much.

"They didn't know how badly damaged we were or they might not have been so alarmed. We took a little more damage when Aberdeen's planetary defenses fired at us for firing at *Tacoma.* Humans. They make lousy neighbors."

Indiw estimated how badly damaged *Katular* had been if Aberdeen's orbitals could shake them up.

Seeing his comprehension, the medic agreed ruefully. "It was even worse than that. So we had to stop firing at *Tacoma* and try something else while reasoning with the humans. What was left of Third Wing decided to mount a boarding party. Crazy people those Thirds.

"By the time the humans on Aberdeen understood what was going on, it was all over. Someone from Third got in and opened *Tacoma*'s landing bay doors. Then our remaining pilots went in, secured the bays, and brought over personnel carriers. I was in the fourth assault wave. We destroyed the Breeders and retook the ship, but it'll be a long time before *Tacoma* will be any use on the line."

"Survivors?" Indiw's stomach tightened. He couldn't possibly be the only survivor—again. No.

"Seventy-six humans counting the badly wounded and the tortured prisoners who may never be sane again. And you."

And what about Chancy? Was she one of the mentally deranged? If she'd even lived through that gravity slam? "*Katular*'s casualties?"

"Heavy. We don't have enough pilots to make half a wing, and in the boarding, we lost a lot of support people. Most of our severely wounded are being cared for at the Ardr facility on Aberdeen, and it's overloaded."

The pain was evaporating, replaced by a languor only the drugged oil could be producing. Fikkhor applied it with broad, efficient strokes, working up Indiw's back as he spoke. There was no hint of resentment in the touch, but Indiw knew it was there, barely masked by professionalism.

Finally, the medic took up a small packet of a different medication and broke it over Indiw's injured horn. Most of the general pain subsided with that. "Sleep now, and you'll be out of here tomorrow. The next day at the latest. Sleep." Indiw could smell the "good riddance" underneath the medic's words.

Four days later Indiw, groomed, polished, and wearing gleaming new straps, faced another Interview panel, a full panel with eight members, but no simultaneous transmission throughout *Katular*.

He hadn't used any scent inhibitor this time, though. He was going to need every communicative ability he owned to get through this. The only remnant of his battle was the bandage on his still aching horn. It was the kind of injury that would probably nag at him for the rest of his life.

But he ignored it. His every moment since Operation Up Theirs had been occupied with thoughts of Chancy and Falstaff. It was only after he'd talked to Chancy via an intership hookup that he understood the name of what they both felt. Bereavement.

He had known the human only for a few days, yet Falstaff's death was felt as a loss as potent as the loss of land. Only to her, it was a very different sort of loss, a sort no Ardr could ever truly comprehend. Yet comprehending it was the key to everything, and Indiw thought he now had a better grasp of what it was the Ardr scholars had missed in their initial study of the human homeworld.

He'd never forget the black-edged shock of knowing the finality of Falstaff's death. The knowing had coursed through and through him and obliterated everything else from thought or knowledge until Chancy had attacked. He still could not sleep without seeing that leg and charred pelvis and feeling his head being pounded into the deck.

Had the Interview board not required him to review the flight recordings and the accounts of the other survivors of the battle for *Tacoma,* Indiw thought, his memory of that time would have eroded away under that surging tide of knowing the death of another as a personal loss.

The only event of the last few days that penetrated that cloud of personal loss was the ceremony the humans had held for their dead pilots. What bodies and fragments of bodies could be identified as *Tacoma*'s pilots had been placed in a black-painted cargo ship decorated with symbols of all the human faiths, sent out into far orbit, and exploded into atoms—as if they'd died in combat. The Admiral who had bestowed the awards on them had committed Falstaff's body to space and his soul to All Mighty God with ancient, traditional words.

The humans had broadcast this ceremony, making it take hours, interviewing members of the crowd gathered on the night side to watch the black-painted coffin ship blossom into a minor sun. The broadcast had visited the worship places of every faith getting tributes from people who lived because of those human heroes who had died. And then they'd done endless interviews of Falstaff's relatives, and they even tracked down Marla Chancy and made her tell of the man she'd loved and almost taken as a relative.

The camera mercilessly tracked her as she broke down again and sobbed out, " . . . and I never told him I'd have willingly had his children!"

Right after that, they'd aired a sequence with Falstaff's eldest nephew, Raymond G. Falstaff, Jr., who said, "I want to be a hero just like Uncle Walt. I want to do something that nobody else would ever do, or could ever do." Falstaff's death had kindled an aspiration toward an ideal. When he understood that, when all he'd observed of Falstaff had finally come together in his mind, Indiw knew the only thing he could say in his own defense.

As his formal Interview got under way, Indiw sat calmly through the reprise of the battle recordings of the quick skirmish with the Hyos on the way to *Tacoma,* the award ceremony where he accepted the Croninwet, the monumental battle with the entire swarm on the way back to *Katular,* and then the combination of *Tacoma*'s log recordings and human eyewitness accounts of the struggle against the Hyos boarding parties.

He answered all the Interviewers' questions about why he'd done what he'd done, most especially why he'd accepted the award. That wasn't difficult to articulate. He'd gone over Trilucca's argument so many times, he had it memorized. It even made a certain sense when translated.

That part of the Interview went quickly because three of the eight Interviewers facing him were the ones who'd gone through this with him before, and the others had studied that

Interview. Then they got into the things he'd done in the battle against the dual swarm after they'd boarded and taken *Tacoma*.

Finally, the eldest among the Interviewers, a male who had affected silver tips on his horns, voiced the matter preying on all their minds. "It would seem you've perfected the technique of fighting human style. Do you intend to become theirs?"

Indiw seized the opening. "To become the first of their conquests among us? To let them domesticate me? The first traitor in all the eons we've struggled against the pack hunters? Do I intend to try to become a pack hunter myself?"

He looked around at the stunned faces, waiting for them to edge over into distaste at his crudeness.

Before anyone could interrupt, Indiw went on, "I'm glad I fought beside them, though I'd prefer never to do it again. I'm glad because I learned something no other Ardr knows, something that couldn't possibly be learned except by fighting in their midst according to their protocols, something we all must know if we're to survive with human neighbors. I learned that humans are no threat whatsoever to us or our way of life."

They stirred as if they'd just discovered a dangerous lunatic in their midst. Indiw rose, commanding their attention with a burst of scent.

At their offended recoil, he stepped closer to the Interview panel, refusing to allow them time to speak.

"The primitive Ardr to whom a spear was high technology lived alone and hunted alone, meeting others only with extreme caution on neutral ground. The history of Ardr civilization is the struggle of those ancient lone hunters to transcend that loner's instinct and make allies of neighbors, to form a group for mutual defense.

"But the primitive human lived in groups—groups of related individuals who knew which ones were their parents, which their children, which the children of their relatives. The history of human civilization is the ongoing struggle to transcend that submersion in the group and emerge from the group as a full individual.

"And they are doing it. We've never been able to understand that before because we never really understood the power of human relationships as motivation. *That* will never be transcended, and in fact it is the very foundation of their concept of Individual. Do you realize that a human defines Self in terms of his children? Or sometimes just the children of a relative? He sees his Self continuing even after he dies, provided his children live on. He sees that because as a child, he, too, aspired to be a continuation of his parents' lives. It's an endless chain back to their very origins.

"That's why Falstaff made that insane charge across the bridge—*Tacoma*'s main dish projector was pointed right at his family—and he *felt* and reacted as if it were pointed at his own Self. Which, for a human, it was.

"Have you been listening to what people have been saying about that suicidal run? That no one else would have had the courage to try it? That it goes down in history with a select few remembered feats? That it sets Falstaff *apart* from the majority, even from the group of pilots? And that he's admired for it? He's admired for setting himself apart from the pack, for distinguishing himself."

The silver-horned one commented, "Yes, we've heard what they've said of Falstaff. They always go on like that when someone has died in battle. They always think the person did it for them."

"You don't see it, do you? We've heard the like over and over, but we've never really understood, we've never really *listened* because humans talk only in vocalizations." He stepped closer and let them get good powerful whiffs of his scent as he summoned the emotions surrounding Falstaff's death. "Shusdim, you said at my last Interview that the term *hero* is derived from their pack mentality. From being pro-claimed a hero, I've learned that's not true. The hero stands out and away from his pack, displaying virtue transcending mere human nature, an ideal virtue few can achieve.

"What does that seem like to you? What stirs us the way a hero stirs them?" With his scent filling the room, Indiw waited for them to work it out.

Finally, Shusdim said, "You mean . . . earning land."

Indiw retreated two steps and took a respectful posture.

Fikkhor asked, "You believe humans are evolving toward the Great Self while we are evolving toward the pack?"

"The key to seeing the truth of this is understanding how human reproductive biology causes them to define Self dif-ferently than we do. And that's the key to understanding everything they do. The only way to learn it is to go among them and smell it yourself. Otherwise it's just something that some possibly deranged person has told you.

"In all the years we've been allied to the Tier, how many Ardr have gone among humans when the humans were in a state of high emotion over their *children,* or their *siblings,* their *spouses,* or their *parents?*" Indiw had to use Tier stand-ard words for no Ardr language held such words.

"Of course these things have been discussed with us, or how would we know of them? Our linguists and xenologists have studied the humans well.

"But how many have made friends with humans?" He wasn't going to mention being dubbed a *drinking buddy.* That would be going too far. "How many have smelled them crying for the love of an absent or endangered relative? How many have smelled them in grief and joy and ferocity until they could understand the human scent codes?"

"You've done that?"

"I was beginning to. I learned enough to know this. Humans are no danger to us. And the more closely they know us, the less danger they'll be. They only conquer or subjugate what they fear, and they only fear what threatens the Self—which *they define* as including relatives, as we define it to include land.

"Keeping that in mind, they become understandable and therefore predictable—no cause for apprehension, for we need never intrude—even by accident—on their defined Self, their territory."

Indiw paused to look around, inhaling the faint traces of inhibited odor from the gathered Interviewers. Even with the sensory handicap of his injured horn, he knew he had comprehension—and even agreement.

And then, one by one, they stood and walked from the room. And as each one passed, he felt the unmistakable laving of acceptance odors. That parcel of land on Sinaha would soon be his.

Moved beyond words, beyond thought or even feeling, Indiw glanced about the empty room. Then he followed his new shipmates out into the passageway.

Because of what had happened here today, things would never be the same for the Ardr. And all because he had chosen to fly with the humans, and met Pilot Commander Walter G. Falstaff, Pit Bull One, a true hero who, all unknowing, had saved the descendants of his human relatives from the ferocity of an all-out war with the Ardr.

ABOUT THE AUTHOR

Daniel R. Kerns loves archery, riflery, deep-sea fishing, gold, photography, hiking, and beachcombing, but not as much as the writings of Hal Clement, Murray Leinster, Isaac Asimov, Edward E. Smith, and Robert Heinlein. He also enjoys vintage movies about war, spies, and intrigue, and the television series *Raven, Highlander,* and *Kung Fu, The Legend Continues.*

The idea for the Ardr universe crystallized at the Air Force commissioning of Daniel's youngest child. The request for a sequel to Pit Bull Squadron instantly produced plot outlines for not one but three more Pit Bull Squadron novels and some ideas for other universes where human meets alien as ally and adversary.

You may reach the author through the publisher's address in the front of this book.